HER CYBORG WARRIORS

INTERSTELLAR BRIDES® PROGRAM: THE
COLONY – 8

GRACE GOODWIN

GET A FREE BOOK!

JOIN MY MAILING LIST TO BE THE FIRST TO KNOW OF NEW
RELEASES, FREE BOOKS, SPECIAL PRICES AND OTHER
AUTHOR GIVEAWAYS.

http://freescifiromance.com

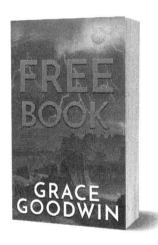

INTERSTELLAR BRIDES® PROGRAM

YOUR mate is out there. Take the test today and discover your perfect match. Are you ready for a sexy alien mate (or two)?

VOLUNTEER NOW!

interstellarbridesprogram.com

1

Umiko "Mikki" Tanaka, Interstellar Brides Processing Center, Earth

WARRIORS SURROUNDED ME, not just the two touching me, but more stood, watching, from the edges of the room. They were chanting something, the deep rumble of combined voices making me feel... safe. It seemed weird, but somehow those warriors were sworn to protect me now. With their lives, if necessary. They were hard-ass alien fighters who battled the Hive. Their protection was no joke. There were nine of them surrounding us, and my mate had chosen them himself, had them swear an oath to protect me no matter what happened to one of my mates.

How I knew this fact, I couldn't say, but the body I was living in for this dream—or whatever it was—didn't care. In fact, she was totally excited by the prospect of having her mates claim her in front of all these witnesses...

Wait? What the hell?

Claim her? With *witnesses?*

Like, stick their cocks in my—no, in *her* body and—

"Do you accept my claim, mate? Do you give yourself to me and my second freely, or do you wish to choose another primary male?"

Primary male? What the hell was going on? And why, oh why, was I so damn hot? One man—no, not a man but an alien, for this was part of the whole testing thing I was going through, I was sure of it now—one alien had his mouth on my nipple, suckling. The other had his hands on my hips, moving lower, positioning his rock-hard cock at the entrance to my pussy as he spoke.

This body—my body, at the moment—was so out-of-control insane for the alien that I—she—squirmed, trying to force him to take her. I arched my back, giving more of my breast to the other alien who knelt beside us. I was surrounded by my mates, their lust for me blasting through my mind in some kind of weird, psychic dream sharing.

I knew what they wanted somehow. I could *feel them* inside my mind. And their lust, their pure, unfiltered need for *me*, was making me—no, her—making *her* lose her damn mind. She was way out of control, and no matter how hard I tried, I couldn't stop her from begging.

"Do it. Take me. God, please," I begged. No, *she* begged. Not me.

The second male released my breast, and I pouted until he moved behind me, his cock sliding along the soft seam of my ass, positioning himself to ensure I would take both of them inside my body at the same time. I wanted that. Badly. Desperately. I was so out of my mind I couldn't think enough to form words. They were mine, these warriors.

Mine. I wanted everyone to know it. I wanted everyone to watch me claim them.

"Mate, you must accept us before we can claim you. Do you accept my claim?"

He wanted me to talk? Again? Was he insane? The body I was in came alive at the command in his voice, my pussy practically pulsing with the need to be filled.

The chanting grew louder, and I wondered just how intently the extra warriors were watching this exhibition in sexual insanity? Me? I wasn't into public displays, but apparently, at the moment, what I wanted didn't matter because the woman whose body I was inhabiting like a ghost spoke up anyway.

"I accept your claim, Warriors."

"Then we claim you in the rite of naming. You are mine, and I shall kill any other warrior who dares to touch you."

Kill?

Wasn't that a bit extreme?

"May the gods witness and protect you." The other warriors, the *watchers,* spoke as one, like in response to some kind of church sermon, as the warrior in front of me thrust deep, impaling me on his cock. I gasped.

Behind me, the second pushed forward, and my body went on tilt as an orgasm threatened to rocket through me. I was going to scream when it happened. I could feel it building in this body's—my—throat.

No.

Just no.

No. No. No.

It wasn't that the two aliens taking me weren't hot as hell. I wanted that orgasm almost as much as I wanted to breathe, but not like this.

I didn't do peep shows, and I didn't get down and dirty in front of other people.

Just no.

I gasped as the second cock filled me. *There.* The orgasm started, and I teetered on the edge, fighting it, holding it back. I would not scream in release in front of—

The scene faded, and I sighed in relief. Thank God. I couldn't do that. I just... no. *No.*

"Better, mate?" A deep voice soothed my frazzled nerves, and I sighed in relief. I knelt on the floor now, in this new dream. My cheek rested on a muscular thigh. I smiled and rubbed my face against him like a cat. God, this was so much better. I was still hot, my body craving his touch, but there was no group of chanting creeps watching two aliens have sex with me. No, claim me. We were alone.

Home.

How I knew that, I had no idea. I accepted the truth of the knowledge as his hand stroked over my hair as if he were petting me. The gesture was soothing, putting my mind at ease. He wasn't ignoring me. The opposite. I felt as if all his attention were solely on me.

When I was ready, when I had calmed from the last bit of insanity, the body I was in knew that they were mine.

They. The aliens. I was still in that weird testing thing. I could feel the strange buzzing in my mind, almost like background white noise trying to break through and enter the dream. Like an annoying alarm clock intruding on my sleep, wrecking the peaceful vibe I had from this big alien caressing me.

This was nice, I had to admit. This was the best I had felt in months. Jail didn't agree with me. Not that it agreed with anyone, but I was not meant to be cooped up in a cage. I needed wind on my face and sun on my back.

But this wasn't me. This was *her*. Some other female. The big alien petting me belonged to her, not me.

I didn't care enough to fight it this time. I let her take me over, allowed her thoughts to become mine.

My work fulfilled me, but it was a heavy load to carry. My thoughts were like tabs on a browser, twenty open at once. I carried stress with me like a bag. I needed time to settle my mind, to transition into an evening at home.

With them.

Them?

I looked around but could see nothing. I *felt* him, felt the soft cushion beneath my cheek shift so I would be more comfortable.

Not a cushion, a man. An alien.

My alien.

No, her alien. She—I—had two of them again.

How could it be? This was a dream. Somehow. I was warm even though I was... holy shit, I was still naked.

I should be appalled. I *was* mad at myself for being like this. I never sat on the floor, subservient to anyone. To make it worse, I was doing it naked.

"Better?" the alien asked. His voice was low and deep, like fudge poured over an ice cream sundae, and I wanted to melt.

I nodded against the first one's leg. This wasn't me. No way. It was a dream. The testing. It had to be a dream, some weird way to assess me for a mate. I wouldn't do this. But I was. I was this woman. Content. It made no sense.

"Yes."

Why was I better? I paused and thought, felt. I'd

returned from whatever job I had, my head filled with the tasks I'd accomplished or that were incomplete. I was familiar with this. My job never ended. Constant pressure, constant deadlines. But I was *her* and I understood. We were the same.

No! I was Mikki. Not this woman.

But I was.

I'd been met with kisses and caresses and had been stripped bare.

I'd let him.

No, it wasn't *him* that had done that. A different him.

A *second* him had taken off every bit of my clothing and led me to sit at the other male's feet.

"Our mate needs a quiet moment to let go of her day," he'd said. He'd pulled me down to nestle on his lap on the floor next to my other mate. So close to both of them, I'd settled my cheek on the second mate's thigh in contented relief. After that, they'd surrounded me. Holding me. Calming me. Petting me.

"Yes, I can see how she is now ready for us." The second male voice. The one whose hands had brushed over me as he'd bared me, as he'd positioned himself to be my body pillow. I shivered with anticipation, knowing they were both so close to me. Anticipation?

What had the guy said? *Our mate?* I had two mates?

"Up, mate. Time to sit on *my* lap." I was easily lifted onto the male's thighs and instead of sitting sideways and tucked into him, I was turned so I straddled him with my back pressed to his chest, facing away. I felt his heat, his strength seep into me.

"So beautiful." Hands came around and caressed my bare skin. My thighs, my belly, my breasts, then lower to my pussy. His fingers slid easily through my eager flesh because I was so wet. Pleasure coursed through me at his touch, my skin instantly heating.

"Yes," I moaned as a finger slipped inside me, curling directly over my G-spot. My eyes were closed, or the dream didn't allow me to see. Hell, who cared if this were real. It felt too good to care. Now there weren't a bunch of gawking warriors ruining my fun.

"Listen to how eager her pussy is," the male who held me said to the other, which meant he was listening to the wet slide of his fingers in and out of my body.

"As it should be." The second male, the one I'd been taken from, agreed at once. I didn't care that he watched me writhe naked on someone else's lap. Someone else's hand between my parted thighs.

The man at my back finger fucked me, the wet sound of my arousal one that couldn't be missed. He spread his knees wider, which only parted my own legs even more. I realized how much smaller I was—or how big he was—when his action made me slide down his body. His cock was hard and thick pressed into my back. He did nothing about it, only continued to tend to me.

I was close to coming from just this, from his hands alone. A whimper escaped, this female knowing it wouldn't be possible. Why was I okay with this? It made no sense. I was at war, my body and mind.

His hand lifted from me, then came down on my pussy in a sharp, wet slap.

I cried out and shook at the sting of it. My clit was on fire and almost painfully hard from the contact. My back arched, and I moaned as the bite of his pussy spanking morphed into the most delicious heat.

Holy shit, that was hot. How? I could feel it all. The sting of the sensual spanking, the way my body took it, loved it. *Needed it.*

"There are no thoughts, mate, nothing in your mind but my touch." His palm cupped my tender flesh before he slid his finger back into me. I was so much wetter than before, no doubt my slick heat covered his hand.

"There is nothing in your mind but the way you feel. How beautiful you are in your pleasure, knowing we are witness to it. That we *give* it to you."

Oh. That made sense. He wasn't taking. He was giving. Or maybe I really, really didn't want to think anymore. I'd done nothing but think and think and think in that damn prison cell. I was so tired of fighting the world. Fighting my fear. Fighting everything and everyone all the damn time.

I stopped fighting the pull of this woman's body as a soft moan escaped her throat. She was like me, tired of thinking. She knew if she let go, she'd be safe with her mates. She *knew* with a level of certainty I had never experienced before—and I wanted that. Badly.

Hands on my parted thighs startled me. "Shh," the other male said. He was between my splayed knees, touching me too. I felt his breath, then his tongue as he licked up my desire from my skin. Oh shit.

Two of them at once? Was I really going to do this? Was she? It wasn't me. Right? This wasn't me.

I'd never had two men touch me at the same time. I'd never considered it as something I'd like. But fuck me, I wanted them. I never wanted this to end.

The hand playing with my pussy moved away, and the air cooled my heated flesh.

Something hard slid over my folds, dipped inside me, then out before moving lower to my—

"Oh!" It was a butt plug, and he'd been coating it with my arousal. I cried out as the object was worked into my bottom. It stretched me, then slid easily into place since it had been well lubricated before I could tell them no. I'd never had anything there except in the first part of the dream. Not in real life. I shouldn't like it, but now... now I didn't want him to take it away. It felt so good. Oh my God, I had something in my ass, and I loved it.

She loved it. This body was on fire and eager for what came next.

"Good mate," the one between my thighs said. "You are opening so beautifully, and we love how responsive you are. Soon we will fuck you together. You want two cocks, don't you, mate?"

"Yes," I moaned as a tongue flicked my clit. My hips rolled into the touch automatically, wanting more.

I wasn't denied. I couldn't describe what he was doing. His mouth, tongue and fingers were all on me, in me, pushing me to orgasm with ruthless skill. Tongue swirls and licks, mouth sucks and kisses, finger fucks and strokes. All of that happened while my back entrance was stretched and filled.

I was panting. Moaning. A hot, sweaty, glorious mess.

"I'm going to come," I shouted. "Oh my God, it's going to be so good."

The mouth immediately moved away, and I reached out to grab his head and put him back.

"No, mate." My nipples were pinched at the same time. Not harshly, but with enough pressure to redirect my focus but keep me hot.

I was lifted up and moved away from the heat at my back, but still seated on the first male's spread thighs. I could feel him opening his pants behind my back, then I was raised once again, pulled closer to his hard body. I felt the thick prod of a cock at the entrance of my pussy as the male in front of me fondled my clit and used his fingers to spread the lips of my pussy open for that cock.

Oh, did I want to have that in me. I knew it was going to be big, bigger than anything I'd ever experienced before. And with the plug...

"Oh my God," I moaned as he slowly lowered me. My feet didn't touch the floor, and I was completely at his mercy. He didn't fit, only opening me up about an inch. I wriggled and shifted, and I took a little more.

His hands gripped my waist and began to lift and lower me, slowly so that I had time to adjust to something so big.

When I was finally sitting upon his thighs once again, I was so full I could barely catch my breath.

"Lean forward," the voice behind me said.

Blindly I set my hands on his knees, palms gripping the rough fabric. He must have opened his pants just enough to get his cock out. And into me. In this position, he settled a little deeper and I moaned.

"Open," the second said, cupping my cheek with his palm, his thumb brushing over my lips, indicating exactly what he wanted. His touch was gentle, caressing my skin in a soothing way that contradicted the demanding tone of his voice.

I did as instructed, opening my mouth, and he guided me forward. Why was I letting him? This was insane. Having sex with a guy was one thing, but being ordered to suck the cock of another at the same time? Why did it make me so hot? Why did I want to *please* him? Since when did I make it a point to please a man?

I *felt* good though. Besides, with that cock deep inside me, I *wanted* to do as he demanded. I wanted to make him lose his mind. I needed them both to feel as good as I did—and I knew, through that strange psychic connection, that he needed me desperately, that he was aching and in pain. He had held himself back to see to my pleasure first.

Behind that desperation and physical lust? Longing. Adoration. Protection. Obsession. Love. I'd never felt anything like this before. My body rode the edge, greedy. On fire. My heart was exploding, the feelings so strong I cried out as I moved forward to claim what was mine, to seal our connection. We three.

I felt the heavy heat of him against my lips, and I licked the tip. The taste of his pre-cum burst on my tongue. Oh yes, he was aroused by me. That drop of essence was all mine, and he was giving it to me. I circled his hardness like an ice cream cone, then took it into my mouth. He was so big I couldn't take all of him, but I tried to. I *wanted* to. My hips began to shift, ready to fuck the cock in my pussy.

I had two cocks in me. Mouth and pussy. This was like a porno, but I was no adult film star. I had two males who desired me and wanted me. I wasn't being used. No, it oddly felt special, decadent. I was the center of these two males' worlds, and they were the heart and soul of mine. They were pleasuring me as I was doing the same to them.

I only thought of them. Their needs. I *felt* them somehow. I knew exactly how much I meant to them. I sensed their pleasure and their lust. I could feel how beautiful I was to both of them. I felt worshipped. Adored. Needed. Protected.

No wonder they'd had me wait quietly, to clear my mind. They deserved my attention, and this connection between us, that I somehow knew was tied to the mysterious collar around my—her—neck, was important enough to be in this moment with them.

They spoke to me, deep murmurs of praise and dirty talk. I felt equally cherished and naughty as they slid their cocks in and out of my body, yet the encounter was so hot. I knew what was to come. I'd seen that in this dream. The claiming.

Either this wasn't normal sex or I'd been doing it wrong. How could it be this incredible, this wild, this dirty and yet feel so good? I was going to come, but I couldn't say it with my mouth full.

From one heartbeat to the next, I just let go, gave over to the pleasure, to the heat, the blinding light, to the bliss as I clamped down my inner muscles on the cock in my pussy and hollowed out my cheeks in sweet suction, eliciting spurts of hot cum into me. Filling me, body and soul.

"Holy shit," I said as I writhed on the hard chair, tugged at my wrists. The orgasm still swept through me, but I knew I was no longer in the dream. It was over. I was in the testing chair alone.

No, not alone, for I blinked my eyes open at the warden who was monitoring my testing. She sat at the utilitarian table, her tablet before her.

I licked my lips, my mouth suddenly dry. I could feel the thick cum as it had jetted onto my tongue, tasted it still. But it hadn't been real.

None of it was real, which suddenly had me on the verge of tears for no logical reason. I'd known the whole time that it was part of the Interstellar Brides testing protocol. I'd *known.* Yet still, this stupid alien technology had gotten into my head, made me *want* things. Made me feel loved. Special. Adored. Like I belonged.

After the last few months of trials and lawyers and a judge glaring at me from behind the bench, not to mention the bitches I'd had to put up with in jail—well, feeling good now was almost cruel. I'd grown jaded, and that testing had taken it all away from me—literally stripped me of all my mental defenses—in a matter of minutes.

Damn it.

"That was insane. What kind of testing was that?" I asked, my voice harsh. Had they done that to humiliate me? Was it some special torture they devised for felons to force them to feel even worse than they had while sitting in a cold prison cell?

"Bride testing," Warden Bisset replied. Her name tag read *Yvonne Bisset*. She was a petite woman who didn't look much older than me, definitely not yet thirty. She was beautiful in a very European way. She had pale blue eyes and dark blonde hair that seemed to curl perfectly all on its own. Her accent was barely there, her English perfect, but I could hear the French influence.

The other woman, the one in charge, was Warden Egara. I looked to her now because of the two, she seemed to know her stuff. They were about the same age, if I had to guess, but Warden Egara had a real no-nonsense vibe about her, which I appreciated. I'd heard enough lies in the courtroom —from both the prosecutor's attorneys and mine—to last a lifetime. I was getting a strong truth vibe from her. Warden Egara.

She was everything Yvonne Bisset was not. Dark brown hair. Gray eyes. Severe expression. Her hair, pulled back into a tight, very restrictive bun, gave her cheekbones a harsh look. She was beautiful as well, but there was something almost tragic about her, where Yvonne Bisset seemed to be free-floating perfection.

Warden Bisset was in training, or so I'd been told before they put me under. She'd be going off to Paris to a new bride testing center where they would send even more criminals into space to be sandwiched between two hot aliens until they forget their own names.

And that's exactly what had happened to me. I forgot I was me and became *her*. Whoever she was. Lucky woman.

I never panicked, and I never lost control. I hadn't survived against the ruthless ocean this long as a world-class surfer by losing control of myself when things got dicey.

But that dream? These two ladies had laid waste to me. Wrecked me. And I was embarrassed and not too happy with myself.

"Do any of the brides sue for harassment after you force them to have sex?"

Warden Bisset whispered disagreeably under her breath, but Warden Egara's dark brow arched. "Were you forced?"

I thought of the dream, the lingering memory of my pussy being crammed full, the burn in my bottom where the plug had been lodged.

Well, shit. It seemed I couldn't make myself lie to her either. "No, but they ordered me to do things."

"They were dominants. Most of the males on other planets will be strong and demanding. The typical alpha male." Warden Bisset's voice implied I would be pleased by this information, as if dominant, bossy aliens were my thing.

Just great. "You didn't answer my question. Was that normal?"

Warden Bisset looked down at her tablet. "Actually I've never had a volunteer who fought the testing so much. Usually test subjects give in and the dream takes over, allowing access to the subconscious to collect the data needed for the perfect match. You, however, had to be subverted to secondary protocol."

"What does that mean?" I didn't even mention the fact that she'd just called me a test subject, like I was a lab rat.

She sighed as if I were a total pain in her backside. I didn't care. I wanted to know what she meant by *secondary protocol*. Did that mean I didn't have a match? That I was abnormal? What?

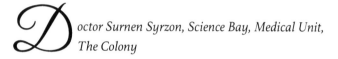

octor Surnen Syrzon, Science Bay, Medical Unit,
The Colony

THE ORGANISM MOVING beneath the microscope twisted and stretched, completely engulfing the healthy Prillon cell floating in the growth medium next to it. Something so tiny, so fascinating, was making warriors sick. It wasn't killing my patients, but the infection was incapacitating strong fighters in their prime. It was my job to identify it, understand it and eradicate it. Not just for here on The Colony, but throughout the Coalition. I was almost there.

"Dr. Surnen? You're needed in transport two." Captain Trax stood at the entrance to my laboratory. He was my chosen second—should I ever be lucky enough to be matched to a female of my own—and a trusted friend. He was also prone to overreaction, his warrior instincts making every matter urgent. He'd grown up on a battleship, been fighting since he was old enough to hold a blaster, and he made decisions in seconds that I preferred to contemplate for a bit longer.

I was a doctor, a researcher. We both followed protocol to the letter—I, as a scientist, he as a ruthless fighter—believing that regulations were what kept us all safe. But the frequent trips I'd been taking to Transport Two to check incoming medical supplies were growing tiresome. I was busy and too close to finalizing the treatment serum that would end this latest sickness to divert my time.

My gaze locked to the infectious cell as it continued devouring the now weakened Prillon cell, I didn't bother lifting my head to respond to Trax. Adding a drop of fluid to the slide, I watched as my serum sample killed the bacteria. I grinned. "Send one of the techs. I'm busy."

His deep exhale was the only indication of his frustration with me. "Surnen, don't be an ass." And his tone. And word choice. "Now. Now would be good."

"Still busy." I had two Prillon warriors in ReGen pods and half a dozen more quarantined in their quarters. Someone else could check off inventory lists.

I expected Trax to leave, to do as I'd requested and drag one of the medical officers down to inspect the new shipment. Instead he stepped farther into the room. "Are you refusing to accompany me to Transport Two?"

"Yes, I fucking am," I snapped. "Go away. I've got eight warriors down with this gods' damned infection already, and I'm finalizing the treatment. As I said, I'm busy. I have more important things to do than inspect the latest shipment to come in."

"Excellent." His happiness stirred my curiosity, and I lifted my chin to look at him over the medical equipment.

"I'm glad you are pleased." I cocked my head toward the door. "Now get out."

"Dr. Surnen of Prillon Prime, as you have refused to arrive at transport to greet your new mate, I officially request the rights and privileges of Primary Male be transferred to me. Computer, please make note of the date and time of this request."

A smooth, feminine voice emanated from a speaker near the door. "Confirmed, Captain Trax. Your request has been processed and sent to Prillon Prime for formal consideration."

"What?" *What the fuck had he just said?*

"Let me know when you are finished playing with your toys, Surnen. You can be *my* second. I'll be taking care of our female while you work. Don't worry about her safety or happiness. I will make sure she is claimed and protected by a Prillon collar and tend to all her needs while you save the universe."

With those final words, he bowed formally, turned on his heel and left me behind my workbench, jaw slack.

What?

My mind stirred slowly. When I worked, every thought, feeling and emotion I had came into sharp focus on the task at hand. The serum sample I'd made could eliminate the need to use ReGen pods to cure the warriors. A single dose of the serum should act as a preventative to further infections. The information and the treatment I would perfect would be uploaded to the Coalition Fleet's medical database and disseminated to the Fleet to assist other warriors who may have human females for brides. As Earth was the only planet that appeared to have females willing to accept the damaged males on The Colony as mates, finding a cure was of paramount importance as the bacteria was a human disease that had adapted to its new environment: nonhumans on The Colony.

With so many planets constantly interacting, the struggle to contain new strains of disease kept me well occupied and was a constant battle within the Coalition Fleet, one I excelled at winning.

I battled what I could fight, using my intellect and ability to focus to cure diseases from all over the galaxy. Other worlds often sent me samples of new organisms and diseases, seeking assistance in understanding and treating them. I would not rot away on this planet feeling sorry for myself. I refused.

I'd spent enough time mourning the deaths of my parents due to my mother's rebellious nature and my two fathers' lack of desire to control her. She'd been fun. I would admit that. My mother had lived life like there was no tomorrow and thrown caution—and regulation—to the stars. They'd all died for it, for my fathers had given in to her every whim.

Because my parents broke Coalition Fleet protocols, I'd become an orphan at twelve. Determined not to allow any others to make the same mistakes or suffer the same consequences, I'd joined the medical job training system on Prillon Prime to learn how to save others. I had no family, few friends, and once I'd been captured and contaminated by the Hive, I knew I never would.

Routine. Purpose. Training. Rules. Regulations. Order. Everything my mother had hated with a fiery passion had been the only things capable of saving me.

I had work to do. Important work. Except...

Surely Trax had been joking about the arrival of a mate.

The arrival of a female match for me was impossible. Fucking impossible. I had taken the matching test, so there was a statistical chance, yet I'd given up hope of having an Interstellar Bride years ago. *Years.*

Still...

"Comms," I called out. "This is Medical. Connect me to Transport Two."

"Connected, Doctor," the comm system replied. Through the speaker I could hear voices. Too many voices for a standard medical supply transport.

"This is Dr. Surnen."

"Surnen? This is Rachel. What the hell are you doing? Why aren't you down here? Hurry up!" The human female was mated to the governor of Base 3 and his second, Captain Ryston. We had not been friendly when she'd first arrived on The Colony. Far from it. But the delivery of her child had earned me her forgiveness for following protocol upon her arrival and insisting on medical exams that she had not wanted.

"Oh my God, this is so exciting. I can't wait to meet her!"

That voice belonged to another human female, Lindsey, if I weren't mistaken. She'd arrived and brought her mother and young son to The Colony and taken an Everian Hunter as her mate. I had delivered her new child as well. I was becoming an obstetrician as much as a bacteriologist.

"What is going on down there?" I asked. My heart began to pound in my chest, but I pushed all excitement back. Surely this was a trick. My mind engaged with difficulty, still fully engrossed in genetic analysis. The switch in thinking was extreme, and hard to accept. A mate. Could it be true?

"Get your ass down here, Doc. We received word of your

match and your mate's imminent arrival. Trax looks like he's about to lose his shit."

Those blunt, crass words could only have come from Kristin—mated to Tyran and Hunt—who had been a law enforcement officer on Earth and still worked with the scouting teams here on the planet. How those two males allowed their mate to place her life in danger on a daily basis, I could neither understand nor condone, but she was not my female to protect. Not my problem, at least until she got herself hurt.

If my female spoke to me in such a tone, I would turn her ass red right before I filled her with my cock.

"Doc? You there?" Kristin asked.

"Yes."

"Your mate. Did you hear those two words come out of my mouth?"

"Yes." I had, but I still didn't believe them. I didn't dare. The only thing that had kept me sane all these years on this wasteland of a planet was resignation. I would serve my purpose and die on this rock. That was my fate.

A mate meant hope. And hope would fucking kill me.

I stood, but my feet remained frozen in place as an explosion of noise, of voices and excited females became a jumble of sound through the comm.

"Dr. Surnen, this is Maxim."

My entire body flooded with relief at the deep, authoritative voice. Finally, an end to this madness. "Yes, Governor."

"This is not a joke," he snapped. "Your mate, Umiki Tanaka from Earth, is listed as being the next inbound transport. Trax is standing here with a blue blanket awaiting her arrival."

Fuck.

Blue was Trax's family color, not mine. Not fucking mine. He'd been serious.

"I received notification, Doctor, that Trax sent a request to Prillon Prime to be assigned Primary Male. Do you wish me to support his claim?"

Fuck that.

"He is my chosen second, and she's mine," I said, walking toward the door... and closer to my mate.

His chuckle would have made me furious if I hadn't been such a stupid ass for the last few minutes. "I thought you might say that."

———

Mikki, Interstellar Brides Processing Center, Earth

THE CORNER of Warden Bisset's mouth tipped up at my question. "All it means, Ms. Tanaka, is that the testing took twice as long as usual. I had to initiate a second simulation, one you would accept, but the data was finally gathered. You have been successfully matched."

I frowned. "I have?" I tried to raise my hand to scratch my head, but I was restrained. "Can you open these up?"

"No. Per protocol, all felons are to remain confined for the duration of the testing and transport. I'm sorry, Ms. Tanaka."

"Call me Mikki. And I'm not going to hurt you." I tipped my chin up. "I'm an environmental biologist. I'm sure that tablet has all my information in it." Sighing, I went on.

"Fine, I was sent to prison, but for destruction of property, not murder."

I'd blown huge holes in a couple of boats. *Empty* boats. Commercial whaling ships that were breaking the international ban. Scientific research, my ass. They gave *real* scientists like me a bad name. Yet that was the excuse they'd used. So what? It was okay for them to go out and kill whales, but putting a hole in the side of an empty boat was worse?

I'd do it again. That was why my parents had let me rot in jail and forced me to make do with a public defender when they had more than enough money to hire an attorney who could have gotten me out on probation.

My parents were big on the law. On rules. Protocol. Duty and family honor. I'd had that lecture so many times I could recite every word both parents would say before they even opened their mouths. They'd been immigrants, afraid to do anything that might rock the boat until they became full citizens. Even after that, the culture they'd grown up in did not approve of rebellious behavior. Family. Honor. Duty. That was everything to them.

I'd refused to back down. In that one way I was very much my father's daughter. What the whaling ships were doing was wrong. The animals they were harming, defenseless. The ocean needed to remain in balance. Even before I got my degree, I'd fought the water itself in surfing competitions, the waves my ultimate competitor. I respected the ocean and everything living in it. Others didn't. Others were destroying our planet, and I was the one in jail for crimes against humanity? What a joke.

Yes, I'd been called every name in the book from tree hugger to hippie to freak. I wasn't any of those things. The corporations dumping chemicals and trash into the ocean, the illegal fishing and whaling operations had done their best to turn my love of the ocean and everything in it into something shameful.

"Regardless of the crime, she must follow protocol, Umiko. My apologies." Warden Egara interjected on the other warden's behalf, as if apologizing was going to make this all right somehow. Again, why was she using my proper name? I wasn't sure if she was purposely being obtuse or just so uptight she didn't know how to talk to people. Judging by the tight bun on her head and the severe expression, I was betting on the latter.

Umiko. *Child of the sea.*

I sighed. "Mikki."

"All right, Ms. Tanaka," Warden Egara agreed but still didn't use my nickname. Cue the eye roll. This woman needed to get a mate of her own and have some hot, freaky, sweaty sex. Speaking of...

"You said I've been matched?" I asked.

Warden Bisset nodded with enthusiasm. "You've been matched to a warrior on The Colony. A male from Prillon Prime. It explains your dream and your sexual preference for two males."

My mouth fell open, and I could feel my cheeks heat. I assumed they knew about the test since she'd been observing, but I thought maybe they were just staring at me lying in the chair. They'd seen me having an orgasm at the end, but having her say it aloud only proved everything I'd done in the dream, everything I *thought* I'd hate, had been witnessed. "How do you know there were two of them? Could you see the dream?" Because that felt like a massive invasion of privacy.

"No. Of course not." Was the lovely Miss Yvonne embarrassed now? Good. "It's simply that to be matched to a warrior from Prillon Prime, you would need to show a desire and a psychological preference for having two mates to protect and care for you."

Okay. This was hard enough. "So, Prillon Prime? That's where I'm going?"

"Brides are matched to a planet first. Then to a specific male. Yours is on The Colony."

"I thought you said two."

She folded her hands in front of her on the table. "You are matched to one, but the Prillon custom of taking a second means you will have two mates. One matched to you, one chosen by your match. Does that make sense?"

So, I was getting one match and his BFF. I could deal with that. I nodded.

She swiped her finger over the tablet. "As I said, your Prillon warrior is living on The Colony. That is where you will transport as soon as the testing is complete."

My eyes widened. "My testing isn't complete? Do I have to do that dream thing again?"

"No. I have a few standard questions to ask, and then we will send you on your way." Warden Bisset looked to Warden Egara for approval, and the other woman nodded.

"Yes. Perfect. Proceed."

"This place, The Colony? What's it like?" I wondered.

Warden Bisset glanced at her tablet and began to read. "The Colony is made of eight sector bases ranging in population from several hundred to several thousand. Residents of each base elect their own governor. The governor of your base, Base 3, is Governor Maxim Rone, a Prillon warrior. At this time Base 3 has seven hundred eighty-three Prillon warriors, twenty-seven Atlans, and three hundred and four fighters from the various other Coalition planets."

No. That wasn't what I meant. "Please, stop. I meant, what is the planet like? Actually, not the planet. If I'm going to Base 3, is it like Earth?"

Warden Bisset tilted her head and flipped her fingers over some images, turning the screen to face me. What I saw looked like Utah, or worse, Arizona. Red. Dry. Nothing but desert and rocks. Zero water.

"Obviously I have not been there, so my geography for that planet is minimal. According to this report, that area is arid. Barren. Desertlike. Rocky. The atmosphere will not sustain human life for long, so you will be required to remain within the base structure unless you wear protective gear."

Was this for real? "Any oceans on the planet? Anywhere?"

"None according to this report."

I was going to a place with no ocean, where I couldn't even go outside without wearing a special space suit? "God is punishing me twice," I mumbled to myself. It was one thing to be trapped in a seven-by-ten-foot concrete cell for the next ten years, unable to touch water more than from a sink or shower, but to go to a planet where there was none? No chance to surf or swim, to see fish again?

"Can I change my mind?" Ten years wasn't that long? Right?

But then what? I'd get out, but I'd be a convicted felon. I would be so out of touch with the industry I wouldn't be able to get another job, despite the fact that I'd worked my ass off to get my master's in environmental science at one of the top programs in the world. I had years of expertise and experience running impact studies, applying for grants. All of it would be for nothing. I'd be an ex-con. Nothing more.

I'd be ten years older and still alone. Always alone.

"For the record, state your name." Warden Bisset hadn't answered my question.

The memories of the dream rushed over me. The gentle touches from my mates. The feeling of contentment and belonging. Of home. The orgasm. The blinding pleasure.

I had to go. I'd figure things out after I got there. They were offering me a happily ever after with two alien warriors who would respect and adore me. Right? Who would make love to me like I was their dream woman. Who would never cheat on me or leave me. I'd be a damn fool to turn that down.

"Mikki Tanaka." It was starting to sink in that this was real. That I was choosing space over Earth. Choosing a barren, desertlike planet over a jail term. I didn't think I could make it ten years without freedom. Would I have it on The Colony with two bossy Prillons?

"Do you have any biological offspring or children for which you are legally responsible?"

"What?" My mind was adrift, thinking about those two aliens and what they'd done to me—her. "No. I don't have kids."

"Are you currently married?"

"No."

"I am required to inform you, Miss Tanaka, that you have thirty days to accept or reject the mate chosen for you by our matching protocols. Remember, there is no returning to Earth. Once you accept the match, you will relinquish your citizenship to Earth and become a citizen of Prillon

Prime, subject to their laws and regulations. If you are not satisfied with the match, you may request a new primary mate within thirty days. You may continue this process until you find a mate who is acceptable."

She swiped the tablet a few more times.

"Your prison sentence is reduced to time served in exchange for your new bride status. As of this moment, you are no longer a citizen of Earth but of Prillon Prime. Do you understand everything I've said?"

"I do," I replied, my voice lacking all the usual intensity.

Holy shit, this was happening. I was going to space. Leaving everything I knew behind. No more ocean. No more fish, whales, waves. No more surfing.

The chair slid backward into an opening in the wall I hadn't even noticed before. Soft blue light engulfed me.

The older warden, Warden Egara, who had been watching and nodding in approval as though Warden Bisset was doing everything right, moved out of the way as the younger woman came to stand beside the opening. "Please remain still for any preparation or body modifications that might be required prior to transfer."

"What?" I began to fight the restraints.

"Ms. Tanaka, please do not resist. You will only hurt yourself."

"Resist what? What body modifications? Aren't two mates enough? Two *bossy* mates?"

"Your testing pulled your deepest desires and wants from your subconscious."

"Those weren't my deepest desires!"

Warden Bisset looked over her shoulder with a helpless smile, and Warden Egara came forward and placed a hand on my forearm, the action oddly calming.

"Weren't they?" she asked. She gave me a soft smile. "Sometimes it is extremely difficult for women as strong as you are to find a mate dominant enough to handle your... umm... needs. Two Prillon warriors as mates will be perfect for you." She gave a little laugh and looked down at her tablet. "Well, ninety-eight percent perfect."

A large needle came out of the wall on a long, metallic arm, and I tried to avoid it until Warden Egara squeezed her hand hard enough that I looked up at her.

The needle stung as it entered my skin, behind the base of my ear, but the process was over as fast as a flu shot.

"We have implanted a very small device into your temporal bone. The device is no larger than a grain of rice. It is called an NPU, or Neural Processing Unit. The device will allow you to understand all languages. Do not be afraid. When you wake, Mikki Tanaka, you will be on The Colony and your mate will be waiting for you."

"Wait!" I called, but the warden just smiled like everything was right as rain and the chair was lowered into a warm, blue bath. My thoughts quieted, but I fought the lethargy stealing over me, realizing this was the last bit of water I'd have on Earth.

"Your processing will begin in three... two... one."

3

M ikki, The Colony, Transport Two

I AWOKE NAKED. Why was I naked? I mean, really? What was the point in that? The hospital gown thing I'd been wearing for the testing wasn't anything to write home about, but at least it had covered me.

The warden had said my mate would be waiting for me. Well, if I was supposed to be mated to three overly excited women, I'd really missed the memo. They didn't look like aliens, although I wasn't sure what alien females looked like, so I guessed them to be from Earth.

They hugged me when I pushed up off the hard floor of the transport pad. They introduced themselves so quickly I had trouble keeping track. Rachel and Lindsey, I heard. Crystal or Christy? Kristin... was the third one? Something like that. At least it appeared I would have some friends out here. Very perky, eager friends. That was good news, because the idea of being claimed by the giant aliens standing around the edges of the room checking me out made me want to curl into a nervous ball, sink to the floor and vomit what little I'd eaten for breakfast all the way across the universe back on Earth.

The alien males were all huge. Epically huge. Like The Mountain on *Game Of Thrones* but handsome and in better clothes. Seven feet tall with sharp features and oddly colored eyes. Their skin tones varied from gold, brown and copper, like they'd been made of earthen elements and metal. They were, to be honest, hot as hell, but I had no idea which one was mine, and no chance to ask questions because the women surrounding me were talking faster than a gaggle of high school cheerleaders at a pep rally.

"Hi! I'm Rachel. My mate is the governor here, and I work in medical, so anything you need, you just find me. Okay?" Rachel hugged me, even though I was naked, which was weird and sweet and, well, weird. She wore a dark green tunic and pants that looked extremely comfortable, a pair of comfy green shoes, and her dark hair was pulled up in some kind of twist. She wore an odd, copper-colored collar around her neck, but she didn't seem to mind it, so I assumed it was the fashion around here.

Rachel seemed kind, and her brown eyes held nothing to make me doubt her. Up close, it was obvious she was human. They all were. Thank God.

The next woman had pixie-cut blonde hair and wore armor, like she was a soldier or police officer of some kind. I didn't think the space gun attached to her hip and thigh was for show. Was she police? Military? She had on one of the strange collars as well, but hers was dark green. I didn't know how this planet worked yet, but she smiled and yanked a blue blanket from the hands of one of the tall, sexy aliens standing near the edge of the platform. She draped it around me, and I thanked her, tugging the ends of it close in front of me. Obviously Rachel was kind, but this woman was sensible. I'd remember that.

"Welcome to the Twilight Zone. I'm Kristin," she said. "I figured you might want to cover up."

"Mikki. Mikki Tanaka. And thanks." I said, gripping the blanket closed.

"Where are you from?" she asked.

"Hawaii."

"Awesome." Kristin raised a brow. "You surf then? Or just love working out? Yeah, sorry, couldn't mistake all those muscles."

Definitely some kind of cop. They were the type to size people up. Threat assessment and all that. She wasn't wrong, but I'd made it easier for her since she'd looked at me bare-assed naked. "Yes to surfing. Two-time world champion, but a long time ago. Now I just do it because I love it. Well... did."

"North Shore? Oahu?" Her eyes grew wide.

"Yes."

"Big waves there."

Again, not wrong. I liked her more every second. "The biggest."

"Nice." Her face looked as if I were describing the most delicious bite of chocolate. A mixture of pleasure and envy. "A fellow adrenaline junkie. I worked for the FBI before I came here. Now I run scouting missions with some of the guys." She tipped her head toward the males in the room.

"Nice," I repeated. We shared a moment of understanding before the pretty blonde standing behind her interrupted. I actually recognized her from some of the videos I'd watched before deciding that being an Interstellar Bride would probably be better than spending a decade in a prison cell.

"Hi. I'm Lindsey." Sweet, blonde, gorgeous with a softness about her that made one want to tell her all their secrets. No collar. So there went the fashion accessory theory.

"I recognize you."

She grinned. "I was a blogger back home. Now I do special interest pieces and handle PR for the guys here. We send videos and interviews back to Earth trying to get more women to volunteer for the Brides Program."

"Yeah, I watched some of those. They were really good."

"Thanks." She blushed, which was endearing. She seemed too nice to be real, but then I was used to working in a lab with a bunch of nerds who spent most of their free time gaming. Or hanging with radicals, hippies that rarely bathed and environmental activists that were just as comfortable tracking wild animals through the woods as they were sitting across from their mothers at the dinner table. Kind, upstanding citizens weren't my usual cup of tea.

Since I hadn't exactly *volunteered* to leave Hawaii, the ocean, my *life*, I wasn't going to tell her that. Admitting I was a convicted felon probably wasn't the best way to start a friendship. "Nice to meet you. I'm Mikki."

We grinned at each other for a moment before one of the giants cleared his throat. I had to tip my head back to look at him. Tall, dark and handsome. Serious expression, equally imposing stance. I'd heard that the aliens who lived on The Colony were soldiers who had been captured in the war, survived their imprisonment with the Hive, but had mechanical features added to their bodies like cyborgs out of a science fiction movie. I hadn't been able to imagine what those integrations would look like. Until now. This guy had a metallic sheen to his skin on his left arm where it peeked out from his sleeve.

"Rachel, perhaps we should allow your new friend to meet her mates." I looked over Lindsey's shoulder as Rachel turned toward the giant with a look on her face I envied. Love. Lust. Adoration. All three. She'd come from Earth and was mated to this Incredible Hulk, and clearly she was happy with the match. Maybe this place would be all right after all.

He had on a collar, too. Copper, just like Rachel's, and I didn't think that was coincidence. I remembered the dream, the mention of collars, of a connection that was special for the wearers.

"Sorry, Maxim," she murmured. "You're right. We were just excited."

The look he gave her? Damn. If a hot guy looked at me like that, I'd melt into a puddle on the floor and beg him to rock my world.

Rachel went to Maxim's side, and he wrapped an arm about her waist. The other ladies moved away from me, each going to a different alien male, matching up. I noticed that both males who surrounded Kristin wore dark green collars that matched hers.

So... they liked to match with their mates here? But why didn't Lindsey have one?

Whatever. Here I was worried about what they were all wearing when I was the one naked. With the crowd that had gathered, I had to assume I was quite the freak show and everyone had come to see what the new girl looked like.

I was plain. Average at best. Always had been. Brown eyes, black hair. I wasn't fashion model material by any stretch of the imagination. My parents were from Japan, and I was short, just like my mother. My skin was clear, my lips were mocha—nipples as well—not the bright, perky pink that I'd envied on girls in high school. But that was a long time ago. I'd made peace with myself since then, teenage angst be damned. I was strong and fast and fucking fearless. If I could ride a twenty-foot wave, I could handle meeting an alien who was supposed to be my perfect match. Right?

Even if he *was* seven feet tall.

"Where's Surnen?" Rachel looked around, confused.

"Who's Surnen?" I asked.

"He's your mate, silly." Lindsay grinned at me like a super-happy *Malibu Barbie*, which was nice but not helpful. I looked to Kristin for answers, but she shrugged. No help there.

Great. I do a beam-me-up-Scotty, travel halfway across the galaxy, and my perfect man doesn't even show up to claim me? Wonderful. Perfect end to a perfect day.

"My apologies, my lady. I am Captain Trax, your second. Dr. Surnen has been delayed by his work. He will meet us later."

"What?" I turned to the alien in question. Trax. Unusual name. He was tall, like all the others, but his skin tone was smooth and rich, like the mahogany desk in my father's office. His hair shone a dark, rusty-colored brownish-red, and his eyes were glowing amber lined with bronze, like tiger eye gemstones. But they weren't cold stone. The way they bored into me made me think of a burning sun, a fire so hot my skin tingled. He wore a uniform with camo shapes on it, but instead of the drab army green, his was black and gray and looked to have the same type of armor Kristin was wearing.

He was some kind of soldier and my other mate was a doctor?

A freaking doctor?

Was God playing more cruel jokes on me? It wasn't fucking funny. I barely tolerated doctors on Earth, hated half of them. In my experience they were either uptight assholes like my father or were players with a God complex who replaced their women every few months like they were disposable toothbrushes with tits—and the bigger the boobs, the better. Size zero waist with a triple-D bra cup? Sure. Totally normal.

I was small. Short. Small ass. Small boobs. If these aliens wanted more than a B-cup, they were out of luck.

Peeking above the collar of Trax's shirt, a shiny, silver metal overlaid his skin. No, not just lying on top, it was part of his neck, embedded, as if it wasn't superficial at all. It reminded me of one of the *Terminator* movies, and I wondered how far down it went on his body. His face was unblemished, if a rich, dark chocolate treat could be considered normal in an alien, but there was a band of silver around his neck and his left ear was made up of the stuff.

He stepped forward and lifted my hand into his. I expected him to raise it to his lips and kiss it or something, like an old-fashioned movie, but he held my palm flat to his and used his thumb to pet me. Just his thumb, running back and forth in a slow, hypnotic rhythm. His touch was gentle, his skin warm. The color contrast between our bodies was impressive. However, the size of his much larger hand holding mine made me feel like I was in *way* over my head here. Mine looked almost childlike in his grasp.

It was time to remember *who* the alien actually was. I was alien to all the males in the room, and they were the aliens to me. It reminded me that *no one* was truly different once the physical was stripped away. The fact that I was standing on an alien world was proof that all living peoples were the same in wants, needs and desires even though outwardly we varied in size and shape and color.

He gave my fingers a squeeze, bringing me from my thoughts. Shivers raced over my skin, and I pulled the blanket tighter around me as he tilted his head in concern.

"Are you cold, mate?"

He was my mate. My second, he'd said. So, this Surnen guy was the one the testing had said was a ninety-eight percent match? The goddamned doctor? Who wasn't here?

"You are my second. My other mate is a doctor?"

He nodded. "That is correct, my lady."

"And he's not here because...?" I wanted to know how this was going to go down right now. No sense getting attached if he couldn't show up to the wedding—or whatever this was. The warden had said I had thirty days to take them or leave them, and if my mate didn't even bother to show up, that sounded like a *leave them* to me.

Behind me, Kristin chuckled. "Oh, this is going to be good."

"Okay. Maxim's right. Let's give them some privacy." Rachel put on what I thought of as the mom voice and started herding everyone out a large door that had slid silently open like in *Star Trek*.

Kristin lingered until I looked up. When our eyes met, she lifted her chin in a silent signal of sisterhood—at least that's how I took it. Her small action assured me that I was all right. She was with me, although I wasn't exactly sure *why* she needed to ensure I knew she had my back. "Surnen can be... difficult," she said. "If you need me to kick his ass, just say the word."

Difficult? Oh, this wasn't good.

"Kristin!" Rachel tugged on her arm, and Kristin allowed the other woman to pull her along with a chuckle.

"I'm not lying," she said as she went through the doorway.

"Tyran and Hunt might have something to say about whose ass you can touch, and ass kicking qualifies," Rachel reminded her.

"Not really," Kristin disagreed. "I don't take orders well. Not when it's ass-kicking time."

"You will touch no one's ass, mate." One of the big guys was talking to her, but he didn't sound mad. He sounded... aroused.

Or maybe I just had sex on the brain. I had mentally prepared myself to be swept off my feet by two aliens and taken immediately to bed to be claimed—as the warden called it.

Their bickering faded as the door slid closed behind them, sealing me inside, naked under a blanket and speaking with a complete stranger who wasn't even my mate. He seemed... gentle. A gentle giant, although I wasn't going to tell him that.

What was I supposed to do now? Go with him? The warden had mentioned this thing about two mates with Prillons, but what did it mean when the guy you were matched to didn't bother to show up?

I turned back to Trax, who still held my hand, his touch so light that I'd nearly forgotten he still held on to me. "The doctor is too busy to meet me. What now?"

He dropped to one knee before me and bent his head. My mouth fell open.

Was he proposing?

"I apologize for Surnen's absence. Please understand when I say I am yours, my lady. Your mate. I will serve and protect you, die to keep you safe. Sacrifice all to make you happy. As a Prillon bride, I ask you now to accept my mating collar. This will connect you to your mates, but will not take on my family color until you formally accept our claim. The collar will keep you safe and inform all the warriors and fighters here on The Colony that you are ours and under our protection."

"I thought you said you were my second."

Trax offered the slightest of shrugs. "As Surnen is not here to be your primary mate, I have petitioned the Prime to grant me that right."

What was he talking about? What right?

Trax pulled something from his uniform and held it out. It was the collar he spoke about, and it was identical to the ones I'd seen around Rachel's and Kristin's necks. But this one was black, metallic, but... not. It was made of some unidentifiable metal. I had no idea how it stayed about one's neck as there was no clasp, but it was an alien thing, so I took it from his hand to have a closer look.

"It's like a wedding ring, but around the neck?"

He looked up, frowned. "I do not know about this ring you speak of, but it is an outward sign that you belong to your mates. Does this... marriage ring form a bond between mates on Earth? Does it form a psychic connection and link your emotions?"

I shook my head. "No."

"How do your males keep their mates happy if they cannot share emotions?"

"They don't." That was a bit rude to all men on Earth, and I heard the bitterness in my voice. Space aliens had no idea what beach bums and surfers considered a relationship. "Well, some of them do. But it's not easy. They have to work at it." My father was a case in point. Very traditional. A surgeon. My mother put up with his stern attitude and alpha-male bullshit and had for more than thirty years. I didn't understand their bond, but I was grateful for it. Their relationship wasn't perfect, but it was solid. I'd never been one of those kids who worried about dealing with a divorce.

"Prepare yourself, mate. You may be surprised by the power of the bond we will share."

"All right." As surprises went, I doubted it could compete with transporting to an alien planet and giving myself to a complete stranger or two. Not just a normal stranger, but an *alien*. Did they even have all the same equipment?

"How do I put it on?"

"First you must accept our claim and grant us thirty days to win your heart."

"You say 'our,' but I haven't met both of you. The doctor was my primary mate, but now he's not?"

"As I said, he is not here, and I have filed a formal claim to be your primary male. *He* shall be my second."

Ooookaaay. I hadn't even met my match, so it was pretty hard to agree to anything. First, second, it didn't matter.

The warden had said I could leave, and I trusted her word. She was too serious about this whole process to lie to me. She'd been human. Rachel, Kristin and Lindsey seemed happy here. I really had nothing to lose. And this guy? He wasn't so bad.

Besides, I really wanted to get out of this room and maybe get some clothes on. I'd expected to be met by my mate and claimed by a big alien hunk who was so hot for me he couldn't wait to kiss me and tell me exactly how perfect and beautiful I was. Instead I'd been met by practically everyone on the base *except* my mate.

Although I couldn't do Trax a disservice. He'd been here. He *was* here, kneeling before me with a collar. He didn't know anything about me and had said that he was mine, not the other way around. I *was* being claimed by a big alien. He was definitely sexy as hell. I had to give him that.

"I accept your claim, Trax. You've got your thirty days." I wasn't going to say the other guy's name. It started with an S? I wasn't sure. All I knew was that the other alien, my *mate,* was *working.* I'd heard that line my entire life from my father. Always too busy for his wife and daughter. Always more important things to do. Always busy trying to save the world.

My father loved me in his own way. I knew he did, even though he and Mom hadn't had my back when I'd gotten arrested. Yeah, that had burned. Still did. Before that, though, it would have been nice to have been placed first in line for his attention without feeling petty and small about it. I knew he saved lives. What was a school play or surfing competition compared to doing surgery on someone who would die without help? Hadn't he known I'd been helping others, too. Whales weren't human, though. To him, it didn't count.

"You honor me, female," he vowed, then stood to his towering height. The smile on his face told me he was pleased. "I will protect you and see to your happiness. You have my word."

So formal. Would he be like that when we were...

No. I couldn't go there. Not yet. The huge bulging of a rock-hard cock was clearly visible behind his uniform pants. I couldn't miss it with his height and my shortness. My eye level was practically *right there*. He *was* hot for me. He wasn't denying it. He wasn't trying to hide it.

He was proud of it.

This hunk was all mine. But only one of them? Why was I disappointed? I'd never even thought about being with two men before taking that stupid bride matching test. The dream had been insane, and it had made me come harder than I ever had in real life. The experience made me realize that being between two men *was* something that made me hot. Especially if one of them was Trax. I had a gorgeous male pledging to be mine forever, and I was bummed out?

Stupid. Clearly I was being an idiot. *Daddy issues* be damned. Maybe the transport had scrambled my emotions. If I said it had been a long day, that was an understatement. There weren't that many women who woke up in a prison cell, were driven to the Bride Processing Center, tested and transported light-years away to be handed off to an alien who basically *owned* her. And all before dinner.

"So, um... what do I do? Just put it around my neck?" I asked, lifting the collar up between us.

"I am happy to assist." Trax moved behind me. Just like in some kind of romantic movie, I held onto the blanket with one hand and lifted my long black hair off my shoulders with the other to give him access.

"You are so beautiful, mate." Those gentle fingers traced a path from shoulder to neck and back again, and my pussy clenched with heat. God, he was lethal all by himself, and he'd only touched me with his fingertips. Maybe this would be okay after all.

If Rachel, Lindsey and Kristin thought Trax was an asshole, I doubted they'd have left me with him.

He reached around, and I felt a slight tingle in my skin as the dark collar touched my neck.

Out of the corner of my eye, I saw the transport room door slide open. "Do not dare, Trax. I am here and she is mine."

The voice was deep and demanding, seemingly used to giving orders and being obeyed. Trax froze momentarily, then leaned close to whisper in my ear. "Your primary male has appeared. I have taunted the beast, mate. Do not fear. Now we shall both enjoy his fury."

I didn't know what he meant, but I stared, wide-eyed as the large alien male came to stand before me. Like Trax, he was tall. Like Trax, he had angular features and was drop-dead gorgeous. That was where the similarities ended. He wore a dark gray cape, the color of pressed steel, with bare feet showing beneath the hem. What I could see of him was golden from head to toe, like a lion. Golden hair, golden skin, eyes a pale gold. He was handsome in a shocking way. Ruthless but not cold. Commanding but not fierce. This guy's hair and eyes were the color of gold glitter, but he wasn't sparkling. He was... fascinating.

"I am Surnen, your mate. I apologize for my lack of presence at your arrival, but I admit, you were a surprise. Not unwanted, certainly. I have been waiting years for you."

His gaze raked over me, although swathed as I was in the blanket, I knew he couldn't see much. Not like Trax, who'd already seen me naked.

"I am honored to be yours," he continued. "You come to me bare, whole and perfect, without any adornments. As is traditional Prillon custom, I come to you the same way." The robe about his shoulders reminded me of a cape from a vampire movie, the fabric looked heavy, formal and covered him from neck to ankles.

He bowed his head and allowed the covering to fall in a pool at his feet.

I gasped.

Surnen was naked. Completely bare-assed naked. His cock was as golden as the rest of him... and *very* happy to see me.

4

aptain Trax Lorvarz

I'D HEARD of the Prillon tradition of presenting oneself to a new mate the way Surnen was now. Naked. Even on our home world, Prillon Prime, the custom was rare as far as I knew, and only practiced by a handful of the oldest, most traditional families. But no one had followed the custom for decades. Especially not in space. *Especially not in the transport room.*

None of the mated Prillons on The Colony had ever done it. We'd have all heard if Maxim had bared himself for Rachel. This was such an old tradition that Surnen was making it new again. Back on Prillon Prime, where there was less danger than on a battleship where I'd been raised, some of the wealthier noble families still followed the old ways. But even they were considered out of touch. Anyone under the age of ninety years would be laughing at Surnen right now.

I was not laughing. I expected Surnen and I to both be very naked—well, perhaps I'd be able to dim the lights so my integrations were hidden, or better yet, leave my shirt on —when we claimed our mate, fucked her until she screamed with pleasure. But this? In the *transport room?*

Our female was not laughing either. She was staring. At Surnen's cock. At his chest. At the silver that streaked his forearm and legs. *He* was not shamed by his integrations. They didn't affect him as mine did me. They didn't cause him a deep sense of panic at the idea of being seen as lesser. Damaged. Worthless.

It was what I'd heard more than once when I'd been a boy growing up on the battleship. Some of our best warriors had been taken, integrated and recovered. But my fathers, even my mother had refused to look them in the eye once it was done. They had been very traditional, had feared that even one touch by the contaminated warriors would somehow infect them—or worse, infect me. Their son. Their dark, perfect warrior son.

I still remembered the day my mother had run toward me and yanked me off my feet, into her arms, and covered my body with her own as she shoved past the contaminated Prillon who'd been showing me how to properly attach my armor.

I'd been eleven, and he'd been a hero of mine for years, one of the fiercest fighters and one of the best pilots. He'd been my idol and a good friend of both of my fathers—until he wasn't.

Once he'd been rescued, my parents, all three of them, refused to speak to him. He'd become a pariah on the ship.

Unseen. Feared. It had taken two days for our battleship to transport him to The Colony.

I'd never forgotten the lesson. Damaged meant worthless. To my mother. My fathers. The entire crew.

When I returned from being a Hive prisoner, my mother had called me once on comms. Standing between my two fathers, who had said nothing, she had cried so hard I could barely understand her words, told me she loved me and good luck on The Colony.

That was it. My fathers had simply nodded as if they were proud of me, wished me luck and signed off as well.

I'd been forgotten by my own family for less integrations than Surnen currently had on display. Mikki was new to us. A human. Small. So small and delicate looking, her black hair like the soft shimmer of a night flower. She was ethereal, still more phantom to me than a real, live female. A dream. Perhaps an apparition.

Then there was the dumb bastard next to me flaunting his integrations and his cock both.

Fuck. He was going to scare her. I'd seen her look at my ear, at the silver integrations circling my neck, and had felt heat creep up my neck and into my face. Shame. She hadn't walked away, but she hadn't seen my shoulders yet either. And I didn't want to lose her or, worse, have her remain and be repulsed once she saw all of me.

I'd planned to fuck her in the dark, to pleasure her until she was too lost in her body's needs to notice the silver imperfections in my flesh. I didn't know how many orgasms that would require, but I was up for the task. As was my cock, rock-hard and weeping under the restrictive uniform I'd worn to hide as much of my contamination as possible.

Yet here was Surnen, fucking ruining everything.

I'd had no idea he would do this. By the gods, she seemed to gasp for breath. His silver hand and wrist were attached to his forearm by twisted silver streaks that ran from his wrist to just below the elbow. He had similar silver streaks running from hips to knees on both legs and also from the backs of his knees to his heels. His face appeared unaffected but for the slight glint of silver in the very backs of his eyes. On Prillon Prime—or Battleship Lorvan, where I had been born, had grown into a warrior and spent several years serving the Coalition Fleet—the hand alone would be enough to frighten a gentle female. But to stand here, streaked in silver? Naked?

I knew transported brides arrived without covering, but I'd assumed it was more because of transport than anything else. Earth was a long fucking way. Although I'd transported hundreds of times, and not once had I lost my clothing or weapons in transit. Perhaps it was specifically a bride protocol? I had no idea, but the glimpses I'd seen of Mikki's petite, naked figure had made my cock instantly hard. The only thing that could dampen my arousal was seeing Surnen bare-assed.

"What are you doing?" I asked him.

His eyes remained on Mikki. "Following Prillon protocol and custom."

"That requires you to prance naked in the transport room?" I could see the young Everian transport tech standing at the control station, looking anywhere but at Surnen. Surnen didn't blink, didn't even blush at the idea of being bare. Or showing our female his contaminated flesh.

"I do not prance. My mate shall know what I am. I will not hide."

I shook my head. "Nothing's hidden. In fact, your cock's

aiming right at her." Why I felt the need to prod Surnen when I had already accomplished my goal of getting him out of his medical lab, I couldn't say. But seeing him this way, out of sorts, unstable, *awake* made me want to push a little further. He'd been behaving like a half-dead corpse for far too long. Years.

This custom he was following was awkward and strange, of course, but had to admit, he'd heard he had a mate and responded. He was presenting himself to her in the only way he knew how. In the most reverent of ways. Odd but reverent. He was trying to do this right, no matter how *wrong* it seemed. This gave me hope that maybe he wasn't as dead inside as I'd begun to suspect.

"I am not ashamed to be attracted to my mate. I am honored by the way she arouses me. You please me, mate," he said, his tone a touch softer, just for her, ensuring she didn't doubt his cock stand. "Trax, put your collar away before I kill you. It is *my* collar she shall wear. You, as well."

I moved from behind Mikki to stand perpendicular to both of them, my collar dangling from my hand at my side. I wanted to see Mikki's face, but I didn't want to turn my back on Surnen. "It's about time you got your head out of your ass," I murmured.

He ignored me, his gaze locked on our female as he spoke. "I shall allow the blanket, for there is a chill in the room, but from now on you shall cover your body in gray and only gray, mate."

Our female's mouth dropped open with an adorable oval shape. As I was not yet familiar with her reactions, I chose to focus on Surnen.

My friend might behave like he had a Viken walking stick up his ass most of the time, but he was not denying his mate. He wanted her. The way his cock dripped pre-cum like a leaky shower tube was plenty of indication. A little prodding, not just from me threatening to make her mine but from the governor over the comm as well—even with a little lying to make him hustle—had him moving now.

He was here. She was his. Ours. I just had to get him to put his clothes back on before she ran, screaming, back to Earth—or to a Prillon mating pair that wasn't... damaged. I wanted to fuck her just as much as he appeared to want to, but it wasn't happening in the transport room with the tech as witness. I didn't think there was a Prillon custom for that, thank the gods.

He didn't spare me a glace, kept his gaze focused squarely on Mikki.

Mikki.

"Trax, you will remove your clothing. Now."

I arched a brow—because no fucking way—and said nothing as Mikki stuttered.

"That's... that's okay." She held up her hand as if to stop me. "He already said hello. Gave me a fancy greeting and all," Mikki commented.

"We shall do this properly," Surnen continued. "Tradition dictates—"

"Tradition doesn't dictate it happens in a transport room," I said. Hopefully he was specific enough in his rule following to agree. "We should take this to your quarters." I cleared my throat. "*Our* quarters."

Surnen's pale brow winged up. "We do not take our female to our private quarters until her medical exam is complete."

"Medical exam? You want to play doctor?" Mikki grabbed the blanket tighter about her and took a small step back. Perhaps it was all females from Earth who didn't like that concept.

Surnen glared at her, and I wanted to punch him. "Yes. You will be examined before we touch you. I must ensure you are healthy after transport. It is my duty."

She shook her head, her dark hair swaying around her shoulders like liquid darkness. I wanted to touch, discover if those black strands were as soft as they looked. Gods, she was beautiful. Perfect.

She shook her head. "Yeah, no. That's not my kink."

I tried not to smile, biting my lip to keep from doing so. She might be tiny, but she was like a little ion blast and I had a feeling she was going to blow up Surnen's rigid routine.

"Kink?" Surnen turned to me, confusion on his face. I lifted my hands helplessly.

"I don't play doctor and patient to get turned on. Sorry, but no. I hate the doctor's office."

"Turned on? Are you currently off?"

Mikki ran her teeth over her upper lip in frustration, and I could not tear my gaze from the sight. "No. I'm not *off*. I mean, medical stuff is not arousing. I know some people like it, but it's just not my thing."

"It is not a sexual encounter, but one meant to confirm you are healthy. We will satisfy you sexually during the exam. Your responsiveness is part of the test."

Her gaze narrowed. "You mean what by that, exactly? What does satisfying me have to do with it?"

"I will assess all your body's responses, including your reaction to sexual stimulation, to ensure you will respond properly and do not have any neurological or other medical issues that we may need to correct."

"And what is considered responding properly?"

"Trax will hold you in place, mate. He may kiss you or stimulate your breasts while I initiate the other examination. I assume you were fitted with the proper body waste regulators before transport. I will confirm the proper placement of the transponders as well as stimulate your clitoris until your body's autonomic response takes over and creates conditions for a proper sexual release."

I wanted to smack Surnen in the back of the head, throw Mikki over my shoulder and take her to bed before the good doctor scared the hell out of her. What the fuck was he playing at? I expected Mikki to shrink into herself, to be intimidated by Surnen's aggressive attitude. Instead she straightened her shoulders, narrowed her gaze and leaned *toward him.*

"Let me get this straight. You want to hook me up to some alien medical gadgets to find out if I can have an orgasm?"

"That is an oversimplified explanation, but yes."

"Don't waste your time, Doc. I can. I really, really can." She looked him over, her gaze moving slowly, and I suddenly wished I were naked as well. "Maybe not with you, but I absolutely have no problems in the orgasm department. I don't need to go to medical to know that."

Surnen's eyes bulged at her calm assurance. She was nothing like Prillon females. Nothing at all.

"The orgasm should please you," he replied. "You will be rewarded for being—"

Our little fireball interrupted the almighty doctor. "For being a good girl? Again, no. And gray isn't really my color. I'm more of a reds and yellows kind of girl. A bit of blue, ocean colors. Sand. Gray, not so much. If you really want me to wear gray every day for the rest of my life, I think I need to trade you in for a new Prillon mate right now."

Surnen's mouth fell open as if he were momentarily stunned. "You will not wear my colors?"

"Not if gray is the only option, no."

"And you will not submit to a standard physical examination?"

"I won't submit, period."

I did my best to hide my smile at the dumbfounded look on Surnen's face. His gaze moved to mine, and he wasted no time in chastising me. "You find our mate's defiance humorous?"

"No. I find *you* humorous. You, arguing with our mate, naked. It appears not everyone in the universe will bow to your rules and regulations."

With Surnen grumbling in frustration, I made myself a warm, safe wall at Mikki's back as he returned his attention to convincing her that he was right.

He was always, always right. Most of the time I didn't question him. He was brilliant, disciplined and honorable. Three reasons I'd agreed to be his second and chosen him as mine—should I have been lucky enough to be matched first. But this female was more exquisite in her defiance than I could have ever imagined.

"My only intention has been to protect and serve you," he explained. "The medical exam is to ensure you are healthy. Covering yourself in gray would notify everyone on Prillon Prime that you are a member of my family, under my protection. For doing my duty, you would now refuse me? Refuse our nearly perfect match and request another male as your primary mate?" Surnen's voice actually shook. I had never seen him so... frantic. Panicked. He hid it well, but I knew this male better than I knew anyone else on The Colony, and I had never seen him this close to losing control. He was stumped.

My gaze whipped to Mikki because I needed to know her answer as well. She had accepted me, but now Surnen truly was her primary male. If she refused him now, I could not make a claim on her, not without dishonoring my friend, and that I would never do. He was an honorable male. He had suffered more than most. I prayed to the gods that Mikki would not deny him. Deny us both.

My breath held as I awaited her answer.

She frowned. "No, you idiot. I just got here, and you're standing around, your huge cock bobbing in the breeze and telling me I have to submit to a medical exam. Not overly romantic."

"Prillons do not require romance."

"Yeah, I can see that." Her eyes lowered to his cock once more.

"I am aroused by you. I find you lovely and desirable. I am not ashamed of my body's reaction to your presence."

"You shouldn't be ashamed, not with that thing." She pointed. "But trust me, if you want to get your hands on me, it's going to be because I'm desired, not diseased. I do not need a stupid medical exam."

Surnen pursed his lips, studied Mikki for a minute. She didn't flinch, didn't even squirm. I was used to his long pauses, his lengthy considerations. But this time the data he processed wasn't scientific. It was emotional, irrational, female, and her happiness and cooperation were on the line. He would have to learn to take emotions and another person's needs and desires into account from now on. I was a rule follower. No question. Any warrior had to follow directives, follow procedures. That was how we remained alive. That was the reason we didn't panic in a battle. Structure and focus were what had kept us all from losing our minds when we'd been held prisoner and tortured by the Hive. I was eager to have a mate who submitted to her warriors, but I wanted her to give herself to us willingly, by choice, because we had earned her trust.

Surnen had to learn that Mikki's trust, her submission to us would be all the more precious if given rather than forced.

He could not make her trust him, nor could he give her orders. She was not part of the Coalition Fleet. She was not military. She held no rank and no position except as his mate. His lady. And mine. Our female had a mind of her own, as he was quickly learning. A warrior would never dream of forcing a female who was unwilling. It simply was not done. If we could not earn her permission, we did not deserve to touch her. That was simple and true. Surnen knew this truth as well as I, and judging by the confused look on his face, he wasn't sure what approach to take with a female who was so... different.

"As I said, and you can see, I am well pleased by you. I find you to be beautiful, desirable, perfect. I wish to show you pleasure and earn the right to claim you forever. I will not ask you to give yourself to us here." Surnen flicked his gaze to mine.

Mikki chewed on her bottom lip, but the look in her eyes was confused. "Look, there was this dream, when I was tested, where they were—" She blushed, the dark rose color starting at the base of her neck and moving upward. I desperately wanted to know what she'd been about to tell us.

Lifting my hand, I placed it on her shoulder so she would feel me. My heat. My protection. My assurance worked, for she took a deep breath and finished her story.

"There was a dream where the woman, the mate, was being claimed by two warriors, and there were a bunch of other warriors standing around the edge of the room chanting or singing or something."

Surnen nodded and I, too, knew to what she referred. "Ah, yes, the formal claiming. Those warriors were chosen as witness to provide additional protection to his mate. It is an honor to be chosen," I answered.

"Really?" Mikki looked up at Surnen from under her lashes. "Well, I rejected that dream, and then Warden Bisset had to send me to a second dream, where the woman was alone with her men. No one else was there. That was much better. I just want to let you know that I don't want that public claiming thing. So I'll stay, and I'll give you your thirty days, but no medical exam and no sex with a bunch of chanting peeping Toms standing around. Those are my conditions."

"You do not wish us to honor you with a formal claiming?" Surnen's shock was making him look ill, his normally golden hue fading to a pallid gray-green.

"Not if allowing you two to fuck me in front of a bunch of strangers is considered an honor."

Surnen cleared his throat. "They are not strangers, and they would not be strangers to you. The warriors chosen are close friends, brothers, family or warriors we trust. You would know them well."

Mikki swayed and tried to take a step back. "Oh, shit. That's even worse. No. No way. I'm not doing that. Are we clear? Because if that's not okay with you, I'll just hit the reset button and forget any of this ever happened. They can get me a new match. And you, too. A woman who will go for that kind of thing."

Surnen's silence stretched, but again Mikki didn't back down or look away. She was fierce, and I was already half in love with her. "Do you always make such demands?" Surnen asked.

"Yes, pretty much." She tilted her head and smiled at him, really smiled, for the first time since her arrival. I witnessed Surnen's reaction and knew this female would be going nowhere. If anything, he wanted her more than he had a few moments ago, as did I. She was passionate, fearless and unafraid to speak of her desires. She would be pure fire in bed, and I could not wait to be burned.

To tame her.

To make her scream our names and beg for more.

I wanted all that fire given to me, surrendered. I wanted her to submit to us willingly, gift us with the passionate spirit we had only glimpsed so far.

"At this moment I wish to share your pleasure with none but Trax, and only in the privacy of our personal quarters," Surnen replied.

Her smile thinned, became wary. "Okay. So no medical exam?"

"I will accept that a medical examination would make you uncomfortable at this time."

"Great. We agree. So now what?"

"Now we will learn what pleases you and brings you pleasure."

She looked at him wide-eyed. "You mean you want to have sex with me right now?"

"Yes." Surnen nodded. "I wish to touch you and give you my seed."

She laughed at that, throaty and deep. "Wow, and I thought I had no filter."

I wasn't being left out of this. "I will show you how much you please me, mate, if that is your desire." It wasn't romance, but I gave her a choice.

She looked between us. "Well, no baby making. Not yet. I told the warden I wasn't ready for that, and she took care of it. But I didn't come all this way for the food. I had one hell of a testing dream, and it made me eager for two cocks. You might as well put those things to good use," Mikki said, pointing at Surnen's cock, then toward mine, which was pressed against my uniform pants. "Yours, too."

She walked toward the exit, clearly done with the conversation. Her head was held high, the blanket tight about her. She had no idea where she was going, but it was clear we would be following this female everywhere and anywhere she wished to go.

5

*M*ikki

OH, good God, teasing that Neanderthal was way too much fun.

At first I hadn't understood the complexities of what Trax was doing with Surnen. The doctor seemed to be a hard-ass—in more ways than one—and needed to be nudged out of what appeared to be a strict routine. My presence must have messed with that, and the guy wasn't sure what to do with himself. Trax had prodded him into action, threatening to claim me as his own.

Yeah, right. Surnen had zero intentions of handing me over to Trax or anyone. I smiled inwardly because while he seemed a tough nut to crack, goading and teasing did the job. Trax hadn't been mean about it. Subtle psychology at work. I was impressed. Hearing Trax's whispered words about *taunting the beast* and *enjoying his fury* was quiet reassurance that made my pussy clench and my knees weak. Who knew I was such a sucker for a bossy, uptight, ramrod stiff, formal, naked—gloriously, hotly, yum-yum naked —alien?

Glancing over my shoulder, I walked toward the door. One golden god—who was tossing his robe back around his shoulders to cover himself—and one frowning, armored warrior hovered protectively right behind me. I had no doubt they would brutalize anyone who even looked at me sideways. This was reassuring and oddly humbling at the same time. They didn't even know me, and yet they weren't going to fuck around.

No one had ever had my back before. I'd been the law breaker, the ballbuster, and that had landed me in jail. I'd only had myself. No one had stood up for me or the reasons behind my actions. Not even my parents. They'd hovered and prodded in equal measure when I was small, but once I'd grown beyond their ability to control, they'd pretty much pretended I didn't exist unless I was sitting at the dinner table with them making small talk or asking my mother about her day. This had been less and less often as I grew more and more rebellious, my actions more dangerous. My father's disapproval had been harder and harder to take, and partly because I realized he was right.

I probably shouldn't have blown a hole in those ships. No, I definitely should not have done what I did. But would I do it again? Perhaps. Yes. Most likely. Even now, how many whales were swimming with their calves because I had broken the law?

My choices were my own, and I'd made peace with them while melting from boredom in that jail cell. I hoped, as I looked at the two fierce aliens hovering behind me now, that they would be another decision I could live with.

My father had tried to turn me into a successful surgeon. My mother had tried to turn me into a submissive wife who served the community. They'd both been protective because I was their only child.

With Surnen and Trax, they didn't need a reason to be protective. The just *were.*

"Stop." Surnen's sharp order caused my feet to stop moving, and I froze in place. "You will not leave this room without a collar, female. It is not safe."

Was this rule for me because Surnen was a bossy fucker or because that was how Prillons did things? There was a difference between his comment about colors and this. Surnen's tone had changed from alpha male to... pure command. This was *not* a request.

The strangest thing was, my body reacted to that tone. A shiver of lust ran down my spine and shot bolts of lightning to my core. I went from wet and aroused—who wouldn't be after staring at these two?—to throbbing with need between one second and the next.

Damn it. My pussy was all about that heated tone. Definitely not what I was expecting. No one talked to me like that. Not even my father.

My mind flashed to the testing dream. Those guys had been commanding, and I'd lost control during the dream. I'd loved how they'd behaved, how they'd handled me.

No, it hadn't been me. It had been a *dream.* But had it? Who had the best orgasm of her life from a *dream?* Why did I secretly love what those dream aliens had said and done? Why did I ache now because of Surnen's similar tone?

Why did I fight not to sway toward Surnen as he walked

over? Why did I crave the heat of his hands as they came to
rest atop my shoulders for the first time? The hard feel,
the... comfort.

"Mate, it is not safe for you to leave this room
unadorned," he said, his voice coming directly behind me.
"Other warriors will interpret the lack of a collar about your
neck as your rejection of the match. They will assume you
are free to take another mate, and will issue a warriors'
challenge. They will try to take you from us."

I glanced over my shoulder at him. "How? I thought the
matching program was it. Done deal for at least thirty days."

"Officially that is true. Within the Coalition, the collar is
a sign of belonging, of protection offered to a female and of
worth when worn by a male."

"Wait. I understand the protection thing, but worth of a
male? That doesn't make sense."

Trax joined Surnen, and I was surrounded by heat, a
wall of alien muscle on each side of me. His hand settled at
the base of my neck in a heavy caress. "No male considers
himself worthy until he has a mate who has chosen to be
with him. It is an honor for us to win your heart and your
trust, Mikki. When you choose us, every male who sees the
collars about our necks will know you found us worthy, that
you chose to love us and gift us with your life and your body.
Prillon warriors fight for the right to claim a bride, and to
woo her."

His words finished me, and I did sway backward, right
into Surnen's heat. "Are you... you can't be serious."

"He speaks true, mate. We will never lie to you."
Surnen's hand dropped from my shoulder to the curve of my
waist to steady me, and I bit my lip to stop the moan from
escaping my throat. Holy shit, these guys were lethal sex

gods. Surnen's other hand moved from my shoulder to stroke the left side of my neck as he spoke gently into my ear. "The collar will remain black until the official claiming, until you accept us as yours and allow us to claim you forever. Until then, the black collar is a known custom. A sign that you are being courted by two powerful, possessive and protective warriors who will destroy anyone who dares to hurt you or try to take you from us."

"Like an engagement ring."

"I do not know this Earth custom, but if it is a sensible comparison to you, then yes. The others will challenge Trax and me to combat in the fighting pits if my collar is not about your neck. You are beautiful, Mikki. Soft. Passionate. Full of fire. They *will* want you." Using a gentle touch, Surnen turned me to face him, and I was oddly disappointed he now wore the long cape. Too bad. His body was… worth admiring.

Trax stood close so I could see both of their earnest expressions as he spoke. "We are contaminated, Mikki. We are not perfect, and we know you could choose to go to another, less damaged warrior in the Fleet. But we want you. We will fight to keep you, if you let us. We will fight to prove our worth, female, if that is your wish. We will fight them all and prove our capture and imprisonment has not hindered our ability to protect you."

He was one hundred percent serious. Shocked, I looked to Surnen. His expression was too serious by far. "Is this true? You'd fight for *me?*"

"Yes. We would be honored to fight for you, if that is your desire." Surnen assured me as Trax stepped forward, his dark skin pulling at me like a magnet. I had to clench my free hand into a fist to keep from touching him, from reaching up and tracing the line of his full lips with my index finger. My tongue.

God, the testing must have broken me, because I was a horny slut. The attraction was instant and insane.

My hand moved almost as if it had a mind of its own, but I pulled back at the last moment, lowering back to my side so as to resist temptation. "I don't know what to say. I don't want either one of you to get hurt."

Trax stared at my hand as if I'd broken something inside him, and my lust mellowed into wanting to comfort him. I was definitely flawed somehow. The mood swings I'd had in the last five minutes were enough proof of that.

"We are not perfect males. We know this to be true," Trax sighed. "The Hive implants make us hideous and contaminated, but they also make us strong. We are not afraid of the challenge if you wish us to prove ourselves."

Hideous? Was he out of his damn mind? I'd seen the silver implants on Surnen's body, and they weren't that bad. Weird, but not a turnoff. Definitely *not* a turnoff. Did Trax think they were that bad? I hadn't seen much of his yet, but it was obvious by his words that he worried about my reaction, that he found the silver bits to be *hideous*.

"None would take you from us, mate, even an Atlan beast," Trax continued. "Do not fear the outcome. We will not be the ones to die in the pits."

"Stop." Who said anything about fighting and dying in pits? "No fighting. No one dies because of me. That's ridiculous."

Surnen stopped caressing my neck, and I realized he'd been touching me the entire time and I had accepted his touch as if it were familiar. Calming.

Mine.

He pulled one of those strange metal collars from a deep pocket in the robe he wore. "Will you accept my mating collar, Umiko Tanaka of Earth? Will you grant me thirty days to win your heart?"

"No one calls me Umiko except my parents, and we don't get along all that well," I grumbled.

"It is your name, and it is beautiful. I have made a formal request, mate. Do you accept my collar and our protection?" Surnen eyed me with a well of patience that was clearly very deep. He was pretty insistent. I had to answer him, or we weren't leaving the transport room. It was either accept the collar or they fought other aliens in something called the pits. I didn't need much imagination to fill in the blanks on that one.

I sighed. "Yes, if you promise to call me Mikki."

He tipped his head. "I give you my oath."

Surnen lifted his hands to my neck, the collar poised above my skin. This time I didn't need to lift my hair, for Trax moved into place behind me and lifted the long, heavy mess off my neck so Surnen could place the collar.

It was black and cool to the touch. It clicked into place, some invisible locking mechanism moving against the back of my spine like a caress. Then, like magic, the collar adjusted itself, shrinking to fit perfectly about my neck. It wasn't heavy, but it was the symbol of a binding oath. Significant, which made it weigh a lot more than it should have.

Both males stared as if hypnotized by the vision of that collar around my neck. As if it were the most amazing thing they'd ever seen.

"Is that it?" I asked, lifting my hand so I could run my fingertips along the edge.

"No. Now we will become one in mind, if not in body." Surnen pulled out two additional collars, offering one to Trax. They both lifted the collars and put them about their necks at the same time.

"Now you will know how important you are to us, mate," Surnen said.

Surnen had only said I had to wear a collar so everyone knew I belonged to them. But he I had assumed they would only put them on if I decided to stay with them permanently. They seemed relieved, as if wanting everyone to know *they* belonged to *me*. I wasn't the only one giving something to this... relationship.

Their collars clicked into place, and it was my turn to stare, admiring them, knowing that the presence of those collars meant they were mine. At least for now.

Mine. These two big aliens were all mine. What a strange and thrilling—

Holy shit.

Lust. Need. Obsession. Protectiveness. Relief. Desire. Fear. Pain. Longing.

Somehow their emotions rolled over me. Through me. I cried out at the intensity of it.

"Control yourself." Surnen barked the order to Trax, and the noise inside my mind quieted to a manageable hum. All the emotions were there but blocked somehow, muted by Surnen's iron will. His presence was like a steel wall in my mind, blocking the wind during a hurricane. I felt the press of Trax's emotions, but Surnen's snapped words had somehow tamed them.

"Thank you," I replied, struggling with the intensity of *feeling.* I'd instinctively reached for Surnen when the overload hit me. Embarrassed, I released the tight grip I had on his forearm. My small words felt inadequate for the level of power he had rolling off him. The level of absolute control. Not only could I see it in his stance, the fierce lines on his face, but I sensed it through the collar. His will was pure steel. Unbending. Unyielding. Unbreakable.

And the alien computer matching thing thought he was the perfect mate for me?

That was just crazy. Wasn't it?

So why did that iron will make me feel so... safe?

"You are mine, Mikki," Surnen stated, focusing once again upon me. He'd heard my wish to be called by my nickname and was honoring his word. Feeling his emotions within me now, I had no doubt that keeping his oath was paramount to him. A matter of honor. "You will not suffer while I can prevent it."

Such simple words, but so powerful an effect on my heart. How did he irritate me and make me want to curl into his lap at the same time?

The idea brought back memories of the testing dream, and another Prillon warrior's lap. Would Surnen's cock feel that good inside me? Would Trax want me to suck him off? Or would they take turns filling me up? Which would I prefer?

I didn't know. Decisions, decisions. All I knew was that the blast of lust from Trax combined with Surnen's iron control had me so hot and needy that I struggled to form words.

Maybe we could just...

I glanced around. Nope. No privacy. The transporter guy was still standing there, pretending to adjust something on the panel in front of him. I wasn't buying the act. A new bride arriving on this planet must be quite an event. If he was like the men back home, he'd be the center of attention later when the rest of the base tried to get details out of him. Me screaming as Surnen and Trax fucked me was not something I wanted as the topic of conversation at dinner tonight. Or any night, for that matter.

"Can we go now?" I didn't want to stand around, thinking about riding their cocks, when they could probably feel me lusting after them through these collars. Now I understood what Trax had meant about sharing emotions. Perhaps this was oversharing? Didn't a woman need to keep *some* secrets? The way they looked at me, with heated gazes, it was obvious they knew exactly how I felt at the moment.

"Yes, mate. We will show you to our private quarters." From one breath to the next, Trax lifted me in his arms, cradling me like I was precious. "Your new home."

Home. That word had meant a lot of different things to me over the years, but I'd never felt at home anywhere but riding a wave or floating in the water. Still, being in his arms and sensing Surnen beside us, I realized perhaps *home* might not be a place. I was ready for whatever came next, especially if it was anything like the testing dream.

6

S *urnen, Personal Quarters, The Colony*

I COULD NOT BELIEVE the female Trax carried into my quarters truly belonged to me. To Trax. To *us.* A female all our own. Forever—if she didn't reject us in the next thirty days.

She'd seen me. All of me. She knew of my Hive integrations. She looked upon them all. I was not the warrior I'd been in my youth. I was still strong. In fact, I was stronger, thanks to the Hive.

But were Trax's fears my own as well? Would this small human reject me because of what I had become? Would she reject Trax for the silver that circled his neck, that made him look... different? I was accustomed to what the Hive had done to me. Trax, however, had never made peace with his integrations, to how he'd changed. Worse, to the way his own family had reacted to his altered visage. Trax was more guarded about his integrations, even on a planet where *everyone* had them.

The interest Mikki had shown, the desire in her gaze, had not been influenced by my needs or wants as her mind had been completely her own. When she'd looked upon me, I had noted no signs of disinterest or disgust. The opposite, in fact. When I bared myself to her, she had not yet been wearing my collar, and I'd watched her closely, saw her gaze scan every inch of me, then stall on my cock. I was eager for her, and she'd seen the evidence. I hadn't lied. How could I when the proof of my desire was evident in the thrust of my cock, the ache in my balls with the need to fill her with my seed? Marking her flesh with love bites wasn't a Prillon custom, but I had a strange urge to do so. The collar around her neck wasn't enough. I wanted the Atlans and Everians on the planet to scent me and Trax on her skin. To know she was well pleasured and protected.

Mine. They were both mine now, Mikki and Trax. My family. Mine to protect. Trax was emotional, aggressive and tended to react without thinking. He was also honorable, strong, nearly as fast as an Everian and absolutely ruthless in battle. He was a good choice as a second for my female, but I had no doubt that it would be up to me to protect them both, to keep us together as a cohesive unit. They were my responsibility and one I was honored to bear. I felt Mikki's delight at the way Trax carried her. My forearm still burned where she'd reached to me for comfort when Trax's emotions had overwhelmed her.

That small action on her part sealed her fate. She had reached for me. Me. That one instinctive act of trust had nearly made me throw her to the ground and fuck her in the transport room. She was mine, utterly and completely mine, whether she knew it or not.

I had no idea of the depth of my possessiveness until now. A fierce protectiveness overcame me. I would not see her harmed. I could not survive something happening to her. Not like what happened to my mother. My fathers hadn't followed protocols on an alien world, and that oversight had killed them all. I could not risk this human's life because I was lax in my role as mate. Emotions I'd held at bay were now appearing. Hope, for one. A second chance at a real life. The deaths of my parents had happened over two decades ago. A different time, long before I joined the Coalition. But my mother's wild innocence and my fathers' tendency to indulge her had changed my path. It had led me here and, ultimately, to Mikki.

I would be fierce for her. I knew nothing else, felt nothing but protectiveness and desire. Even greed. Yes, I was greedy for this female to be all mine. I would share her only with Trax.

The collars' connection between all three of us was intense. I had heard of what would happen when we wore them, but the reality was beyond expectations. I'd never had this mental bond with another. I could feel Trax's eagerness for our mate amplifying my own desire. His thrill of having her here. His worry that she might reject him. That he might fail me as a second.

I hoped his worry would prove futile, but his doubts had become mine and contributed to my decision to bare myself to our female upon our first meeting, as had been done in the old ways. I wanted her to see me, all of me, silver and gold, Prillon and Hive, and know the damaged male she would have as her own.

If she were to reject me, I would survive the pain if the act was done early, at first sight, before I knew anything about her.

Now, with my collar around her neck, I was fucked, because Mikki's feelings couldn't be hidden. While I could not see her face tucked into Trax's body, I didn't need to read her emotions. I *felt* them.

She was overwhelmed. Thrilled. Eager. Nervous. Aroused.

Thank fuck for the last because I would get inside her. Soon.

Very soon.

The emotions I did not sense were disgust. Disdain. Judgment. She appeared to have taken one look at both of us and accepted us as we were.

I failed to sense possessiveness. Longing. Love. The lack caused my chest to ache, and I wasn't sure when I'd become so weak as to need those things from a small human female.

The moment I'd seen her, that was when the dagger had landed in my heart. Her banter had twisted the blade, her desire shoving it deeper within me. We must win her over. To lose her now would break me in a way I could not have imagined.

"This is where you live?" she asked, looking around my sparse quarters once Trax put her down.

"This is where *we* live," I corrected.

"I will forfeit my quarters today and move my things here, to be with you, mate," Trax said.

I paused and took in the space as she might. Plain walls the color of warm desert sand. Simple furnishings of a table and chairs for dining. In the corner, a comfortable seat where I read in the evenings. Another long seating area for guests, which had not once been used. Until now. Now it was needed, although I would not mind if Mikki sat upon my lap.

Or at my feet.

The view from the window was of the arid, barren section of the planet. Base 3, our home, was not in the most welcoming of environments. Red and brown rock scattered in aggressive formations as far as the eye could see. Small, spindly plants fought for purchase in the nearly nonexistent soil, clinging to the rocks with hooklike barbs that burrowed into the hard surface beneath. There was no water, no kindness in the landscape. The window was not in place so I could admire the austere beauty of the planet, but to keep my small living space from feeling claustrophobic. But it did nothing to improve the lack of comfort in my personal space.

Attached was a room with an S-Gen station and a huge bed. When The Colony began accepting brides, the governor had ordered all quarters to be ready for mates. For Prillons, that meant a bed for three. There was also a bathing room. Nothing else. Did Earth women require more? I knew not. I would see to her every need myself and would provide anything tangible she required from the S-Gen machine.

Everything else, Trax and I would see to ourselves.

Like her pleasure.

"We are as unaccustomed to the match as you," Trax said, sliding a hand over her hair. "We are given only a few minutes notice prior to your transport that we are mated."

Her unease increased as she looked around.

"You are worried, Mikki. Upset. I do not understand this

reaction. Everything you see belongs to you now, and what you do not have, we will provide," I told her.

"These collars might be a little... intense, but you can't control my emotions." A little V formed in her brow at his words. "If you came fourteen light-years to become a mate to two strange aliens, leaving everything you knew behind, wouldn't you be a little worried?"

Her ability to defy me was astounding. No one contradicted me. This defiance was frustrating and bothersome, but now that I could sense her emotions, I recognized it as a defense mechanism. An emotional response she used to protect herself. She wasn't being difficult simply to irritate me. She *wanted* this mating to work. However, she wouldn't comply when she didn't understand. Her worries were legitimate and not wholly unfounded. Neither Trax nor I were used to bending to accommodate others.

"It is our job to remove these worries. One at a time until they no longer exist," I told her, moving to stand directly at her side. I stroked her hair now, felt the silky strands glide through my fingers with an obsessiveness I'd never felt before. Once I sensed her satisfaction at the touch, I realized I could do this, and this alone, for hours.

I needed control, but I also needed to soothe. To ease her burdens. In this moment there was nothing I wanted more.

"Why did you volunteer to be a bride?" Trax asked.

I heard her intake of breath, felt her defensiveness return in a blockade of wild emotions, and she closed her mouth so tightly her jaw muscles clenched and her lips formed a small line.

"Mate," I said. "You will answer the question."

The walls she'd erected grew even stronger, and Trax looked to me, his eyes narrowed. Somehow that was the wrong thing to say to our female.

Mikki stepped back, away from my touch, and paced the room. I dropped my hand to my side, oddly hurt by the small rejection. As soon as the thought passed through me, Mikki's gaze darted to my face, her expression surprised, and her emotion one of reluctance and confusion. Was she surprised to know that I desired to touch her? That I needed her to accept the contact? My protection? My life? I was hers now. I understood that completely in this moment. How could I make her realize what that truly meant? What she meant to both Trax and myself?

"Perhaps instead of giving us your reasons, you will tell us why you do not wish to share them," Trax said, his voice calm. Slow. Low.

She paused, looked his way.

"I can feel your disappointment," she replied, tugging at the collar. "I'm not sure I like these things."

"There shall be no secrets between us," I countered.

Trax sighed when Mikki's eyes flared and a burst of anger came through my collar. I knew Trax had felt it as well. Everything I said was wrong with this female.

Moving to the long couch, Trax sat down, patted his knee. "I have seen the other human females sit upon their mates' laps, and it has brought them joy. Contentment, perhaps. Come."

She eyed him. He gazed upon her but said nothing more. I watched, sensing that this was a scientific experiment of its own. It was an interaction between species, human and Prillon. It was also the newfound connection between mates.

"Please, Mikki. You have nothing to fear from me." Trax's voice was far more soothing than I could have managed at the moment, and I was relieved when she complied.

Slowly Mikki went over to him and stood between his parted thighs, wrapped in the blanket. His large hands curved around her hip and he pulled her forward to sit sideways upon his knee, then held her close.

Her back went ramrod straight, but she allowed him to hold her.

Interesting. Her hesitation was strong, but then his sense of satisfaction hit both Mikki and me through the collar. She relaxed and leaned into him, settling her head on his shoulder. Her relief was palpable as well, and I resisted the urge to pace with my frustration. She was a difficult female, unlike any other I had encountered, and I was having no luck figuring out how to make her obey.

And more, how to make her want me. Accept me. Accept my claim as her mate. While we'd just met, it was hard to be patient. Didn't she understand how long I'd waited for her?

If she were a Prillon female, I would be balls-deep already, my cock making her writhe and scream with pleasure. A Prillon female would expect it, but these human females were... difficult.

"I am proud of you, mate," Trax said. "I like the feel of you in my arms."

"I'm just skin and bones," she muttered, but her pleasure at his praise came through the collars clearly. Perhaps that was the key to winning her over? I was not an idiot. I could think of many ways to praise this female.

"You are perfect," I said, coming over to join them. I dropped to my knees before her.

When she remained still, accepting of our presence,

Trax slowly lowered the blanket from about her shoulders so it pooled in the crooks of her elbows. Her breasts were still covered, but barely. Only the soft top swells were visible.

She sucked in a breath but didn't resist. I felt her arousal, her nervousness. Neither were disappointing.

"You have not answered our questions," I said, mimicking the same easy tone that Trax had used. I raised my hand and placed my palm over the bare skin on her shoulder. She groaned and closed her eyes as I caressed her.

So soft. Softer than anything I'd imagined. "Why did you decide to be a bride?"

She opened her eyes and looked at me, her gaze locking with mine for the first time since her arrival, and I felt flayed to the bone. Bare. More naked than I'd ever been in my existence.

"I was tired of fighting."

"Fighting what or whom? Name them and I will destroy them for you." The offer was not made in jest, and she shook her head.

I was damaged, mentally rigid. I'd survived by becoming harsh, by locking emotion away until I felt nothing. I'd had an innocent heart, had loved the wildness in my mother and imagined that my mate would be exactly like her when I grew into a warrior. Her death, the deaths of my fathers had taken me from a perfect world to one of constant fear and struggle. I'd been an orphan in the training program. No visitors. No care packages from home. No holiday celebrations or words of encouragement when I'd needed them. I had learned to rely on myself and closed off all feelings. I'd vowed never to be so vulnerable again, never to allow sentiment to overcome sense. I adopted the life of a warrior and a doctor and embraced the steady, reliable structure and protocols to make me strong. The Fleet, practicing medicine, created boundaries, gave me something to live by when I couldn't even think. The Fleet had saved me, and I'd learned to crave order and stability. Duty. Schedules and protocols. That rigid structure had protected my sanity, and I would ensure it kept Mikki safe.

"Myself." One look in her eyes and she sliced me open like a blade, my heart and soul bloody and scarred and barely beating. Fuck, I could feel. I could hope again. To have something, a connection, a bond. Love. A mate who brought me back from... nothing.

The collars were designed to help Prillon males please their mates, keep them happy. But in that moment they were giving her everything she needed to conquer *me*. I'd kept my past buried so deeply I tried not to think of my parents at all. But I'd never had the collars, never felt so exposed.

"Why would you be fighting yourself?" Trax asked, his voice quiet.

Instead of answering the question, she changed the subject. "I don't want to talk about it now."

"All right, mate, we will save that conversation for later. After you have been well pleasured."

A spike of lust hit both Trax and me, and I saw his eyes darken in response. Our mate's body was making demands, and I would see to her now.

While I was on my knees, I was still taller. Her dark eyes held so many things, but her emotions shifted too rapidly for me to understand what I should do next. Kiss her? Fuck her? Talk to her? She was a puzzle I had no idea how to solve.

I dropped the cloak again, baring myself to her once

more. "You saw the integrations. You know I am not a perfect warrior."

Her gaze searched my imperfections, traced the long lines of silver that were embedded in my skin.

"You got those from being a prisoner?"

I nodded.

She looked to Trax, but he made no attempt to remove his uniform shirt so she could see what the Hive had done to him. His integrations were completely different from mine, but no less shocking to look upon. As a doctor, I'd seen more of everyone's integrations than most.

"I was a prisoner, too," she offered. She'd chosen to share after all. "But not because I was a soldier. I broke the law. I went to jail. It was either spend ten years locked up in a prison cell or take a chance and come here."

"You broke the laws of your planet," I said, stiffening. This small female defied the laws of her world? I could not believe her capable of it. How the hell was I matched to someone who could do such a thing?

"See? You're not happy. I knew this would happen if I told you the truth." She tried to wriggle off Trax's lap, but he wouldn't allow it, his arms tightening to hold her in place.

It was my emotions she responded to. I had to tame them. "Mate, I live for rules. I don't abide by breaking them. In the Coalition Fleet, it could lead to death, and not just your own. Tell us what you did."

I had to know.

She sighed and rolled her head around on top of her neck, as if stretching the tight muscles I had felt beneath my palm would make speaking easier. "I blew holes in a couple of whaling ships."

"What is this type of ship? We do not have them in the

Coalition Fleet." Trax pulled her back against his chest, and I rubbed her soft shoulder with my thumb. Gently. It appeared she had forgotten I was touching her. I had no intention of reminding her and risking rejection.

"It's an Earth ship, made to sail on water, not a spaceship. They use the ships to hunt and kill whales. They are peaceful animals that have been hunted to the brink of extinction. I could not allow that to happen. There was no one on board the ship. My intention was to damage the ship, not to hurt anyone."

Her words came out in a rush, as if she'd held them in for so long that they all fell out at once.

"You were defending the weak from those who would harm them?" Trax asked.

She shrugged. "In a way, yes. The whales can't fight back. They don't have weapons. It's not a fair fight. I had to try to save them."

"I do not know these whales."

"They are animals that live in water. Beneath it. They do not have arms or legs, only fins. They are large, larger than your quarters. They are gentle, beautiful creatures."

"Are they intelligent creatures?" I asked.

"Yes. Very. They just can't speak for themselves."

"What you did was honorable," I said.

"I agree," Trax added.

She shook her head. "I destroyed property. I was in jail for it and chose the Brides Program instead of a ten-year sentence."

"Ten years' punishment for protecting the weak and defenseless?" That sounded ridiculous. What kind of planet was Earth?

"Yes."

The collars were a powerful thing. I sensed so much and knew what was required.

I stood, moved to a hidden compartment near the bedchamber. I had not planned to ever claim a mate, but I was a doctor. I was prepared. Always.

I removed the box and caught Trax's eye, felt his excitement as he recognized what I held. "What you did was honorable," I repeated. "Defending the weak, the vulnerable. Both are excellent traits. Traits we want in a mate. I am proud of you."

I felt her surprise and... pleasure at the praise. Not physical pleasure, but a sense of reassurance. I wasn't done.

"You please me, mate."

"Us," Trax said.

I looked to him. Nodded. "Now it is time for *us* to show you how two Prillon warriors pleasure their mate."

 *ikki*

I NODDED. I'd bared my secrets just as Surnen had bared his body, and they hadn't found me lacking. In fact, they were happy with me. So much so that I sensed their increased arousal. I practically melted under their praise but got wet from the desire I felt through the collars.

Trax loosened his hold on me, and I stood, let the blanket drop to my feet.

Surnen took in my body, his eyes going wide. "What... female... I do not understand what I am seeing. Why does it appear as if you are wearing clothing when you are not?"

I glanced down at myself. I looked the same. Same arms, legs, boobs. Oh. "You mean the tan lines?"

"Tan lines," Surnen repeated, pointing his finger at my torso.

I stifled a smile. "Being exposed to Earth's sun changes

the pigment of my skin." I explained how my bathing suit had covered certain areas.

Surnen continued to eye me as he processed the concept. Then he took a deep breath as if he were trying to scent my need in the air. "Are you wet for me, Mikki?"

I could tell him the truth of this. He'd find out soon enough. He could *feel* how aroused I was through the dang collars. "Yes."

Not just wet; my body's need was sliding down my inner thighs.

At my back, Trax shuddered and a wave of lust—his lust—blasted through my mind. I whimpered. Surnen held still. Steady. Unmoving, even though I could sense his own need.

"How were the two Prillon males pleasuring the female in your testing dream?" Trax asked.

Surnen set his hand at the nape of my neck and led me into the bedroom. Once there he released his hold and sat on the side of the huge bed. It was larger than any I'd seen on Earth, large enough to fit three people. Hell, bigger because Trax and Surnen weren't human. They were seven feet plus of hot alien.

"One put his mouth on her pussy," I said, meeting Surnen's eyes. "Then he stopped, and the second male fucked her. She sucked off the first at the same time."

"What about her ass?" Trax asked. It seemed he liked dirty talk. His hand slid up and down my bare spine until it settled on my bottom. I gasped, wondering what he'd do.

He did nothing except caress one cheek, cupping it.

"They put a plug in her." I couldn't miss the breathy sound of my voice.

"You want that," Surnen said. "Something in your ass."

I nodded.

"We know." From behind, Trax's hand dipped between my thighs, his fingers slipping over my pussy. I spread my legs for him, realized how bold the action was and tried to close them. He stopped me with a little spank to my ass as he laughed. "We know because we are your mates. Surnen was your perfect match. He knows your desires because they are his, too. Mine, as well."

I was having a hard time following with the way his hand played. I was so wet it coated his palm, made his passage slick and sensitive. He did nothing but stroke me, learning my pussy... on the outside. Trax's other arm came around me and cupped a breast, his fingers tugging and playing with my nipple. My head fell back and rested against his chest.

Surnen held up the plug as he watched what Trax was doing to me. "This is a Prillon training plug that prepares new mates for the official claiming. When she takes both her mates at the same time."

What Trax was doing wasn't enough. I needed more. I needed Surnen to touch me, too. After the dream, one male wasn't going to cut it. I'd never considered it before the testing, but now I didn't want anything else. I felt cheated without a second set of hands on my body.

"Please," I whimpered.

Surnen smiled. Actually *smiled* and he was gorgeous. His golden skin, pale eyes, huge body. All of it was transformed with his satisfaction. "What a good little mate. You beg so beautifully."

Oh. My. God. I had.

Curling his finger, he beckoned me over. Trax's hands dropped away, and I stepped toward Surnen, close enough for him to wrap an arm around me and pull me the rest of the way to him so I stood between his parted knees. With our height difference—even with him sitting on the bed— his mouth was in line with my breasts. Leaning forward, he took one into his mouth, kissed the nipple, then sucked, drawing on it in hard pulls.

I gasped, my hands going to his hair and tangling in the silky strands.

He alternated between my breasts, worshipping them. They were small, I was no playboy centerfold but he focused on them. Only them. Mouth, hands. Sucks, licks, laves, tugs. I had no idea they were so sensitive, that they could make me so hot.

A hand went about my waist, pulled my hips backward. Trax. The motion shifted me away from Surnen, and he lifted his head. His mouth was red and slick from his actions. His gaze, while pale, held heat. Need.

Trax's hand settled on my bottom, and he pulled, opening me up. My eyes flared wide, and I stiffened at the hard prod of something at my back entrance. I glanced over my shoulder, and Trax looked my way and winked.

Winked! I had no idea aliens did something like that, but it was a hint at his playfulness. The press of the plug against my virgin entrance was a reminder that he wasn't to be denied.

Surnen set his fingers to my chin and turned my face back toward his. "I shall watch you as you take a plug for the first time."

I gasped as the very tip of the plug opened me up, but felt a gush of liquid into me; then the hard object slipped right in. I was unused to the sensation of something going *in* there, being stretched open, kept open. It burned and was uncomfortable but didn't hurt. It had to have been lube I felt, for it eased the way and—

"Oh my God," I moaned.

Surnen's smile widened, his gaze roving all over my face, dropping to my breasts, then back up. "It vibrates."

"I... yes. I know," I breathed. Trax hadn't removed his hand from my bottom, and I knew he was behind me. Watching. He could see the thing in me, how it filled me. It was so dirty. Naughty, even. He could also see my pussy, how wet I was. I was completely exposed, completely vulnerable to them.

And they hadn't hurt me. They hadn't laughed. Made fun. Shamed me for having something... *wanting* something in my ass. They were aroused by it. I couldn't miss Surnen's cock, the way it still weeped pre-cum, how the color of it was darker than the rest of his skin. He was hard, almost impossibly tight. His balls were large and heavy, pendulous and full of cum.

Oh God, all of it was for me. Sooo hot.

What was in that lube? All of a sudden I was a hussy with the libido of a porn star. I wanted it. Wanted the plug in my ass, especially if it kept vibrating. I wanted Surnen's huge cock in my pussy. As for Trax... he could have my mouth. Just. Like. The. Dream.

"Please," I begged again.

"Do you decide how you'll be fucked, mate?" Surnen asked again. How could he be so controlled sitting there when I felt his need, so potent and ruthless through the collar?

I shook my head. "No, but I need—"

"We know what you need," he replied.

Damn his calmness!

Trax's hand slid around my hip in front and between my legs. Two fingers slipped into me. "She's ready."

"I've *been* ready," I snapped, pushed to my limits. And so fast. I had no idea I was so sensitive, so needy.

His fingers pulled from me, and his hand slapped down on my pussy. The slap stung my wet lips, but a burst of hot pleasure seared my clit. I gasped.

"Mate," Trax warned but said nothing more. His hand stroked over the delicate folds he'd just spanked with a gentle touch.

I whimpered. My skin was damp with sweat, and I was losing control. The thing in my bottom stopped vibrating and I moaned, but then something else happened. It grew.

"What... what's it doing?"

I shifted my hips, squirmed as it sank a little deeper into me, as a cock would, and thickened.

"Besides preparing you to be claimed by your mates? It's making you hotter. Wetter."

Yeah, it was.

Surnen dropped back onto the bed so he lay upon it, his knees bent and feet on the floor.

"Climb on, mate," Trax said, leaning down and speaking right by my ear. "Surnen is desperate for the tight clench of your pussy around his cock."

I felt a wave of lust swamp me. Surnen had been holding back. Somehow he'd kept his heat and need under control. Until now.

I licked my lips, studied Surnen. His body was so big, so powerful with muscles. This guy didn't go to a gym. He must move rocks or something for exercise. There wasn't an ounce of fat on him. The integrations, that silver embedded beneath his skin, only made him even hotter. God, what he'd gone through. They were a reminder he was a warrior. A fighter. And I got to climb onto his body and use it for my pleasure.

At their command.

What a dichotomy.

I wasn't going to be told again. I wasn't going to argue. I wasn't going to do anything but crawl up onto the bed, then throw a leg over Surnen's broad chest and straddle him.

Surnen's hands settled on my hips, lifted me as if I were a feather so I hovered over his cock, then lowered me onto it. The tip stretched me open and I moaned. He was so big, especially with the plug in me.

Holy shit. It was like the dream. Only better. So, so, so much better. I could feel Surnen. I could see him. Breathe him. He was mine. This wasn't a dream. It was real and his cock was going in... in and all the way in until I sat upon his lap.

"Good mate," he murmured. The sensation of being stretched open was combined with *his* feelings. I even sensed how Trax watched, how the sight of us together pleased him. I looked over my shoulder at him. His clothes were still on, but his pants were open, lowered enough so his cock was out. I looked up at him as he stroked himself. I sensed his desire but also his insecurities, which made no sense. Not with the huge thing he gripped.

"Aren't you going to take your clothes off?" I asked. It was hard to talk, hard to think with Surnen deep inside me.

Trax shook his head slowly, taking me in straddling Surnen.

"Trax, get your fucking uniform off," Surnen snapped.

"No," Trax replied.

All of a sudden I felt things, emotions I couldn't

understand. I had to figure it out though, even like this, even with a cock in my pussy and a plug in my ass.

"Trax, what's wrong?"

He looked away. Sighed. "I do not wish to disgust you with my integrations."

Surnen swore under his breath.

I frowned. This huge warrior had insecurities about his body? Was he insane? No, he was afraid. It was my job—and probably only mine—to rid him of that.

I pointed to the left side of my torso. "See this scar? Thirty-four stitches from slamming into coral." I dropped my hand to my knee. "ACL repair. Isn't that scar huge? Then there's this." I turned away from Trax, and Surnen shifted inside me. He groaned. My eyes fell closed at how blissful he felt. "On my back. I can't see it, but I was at work and fell on a site. Hit a rotting log that had a knot exposed. I won't tell you how bad that was."

"Work? What work do you do?" Trax asked.

I pursed my lips. "I'm sitting on Surnen's cock and you're asking about my job? Trax, I promise I shall not be… bothered by your integrations. If I can stand Surnen's surliness"—the man in question growled and grabbed my hips—"then whatever you're packing under that clothing will not bother me."

A slight smile turned up the corner of his mouth.

I paused, stared at his cock he was still absently stroking and let him feel the blast of desire through the collars.

A sound rumbled from his chest, and he tugged the shirt up and over his head. Yes, he had silver like Surnen. Trax's was about his neck beneath the collar and onto his broad shoulders, his pecs. Up the side of his neck to his ear.

Whatever. The man was a god. Integrations or not, he

was hot. H.O.T. His skin was the color of cinnamon, a rusty tone. I'd never seen skin that color before, ever. In the room lighting, it almost gleamed. So did the pre-cum beading at the tip of his cock. He grasped the base, stroked himself, using his thumb to rub the fluid into his skin.

"Want to tell me how you got them?" I asked.

His eyes narrowed. His jaw clenched. "Absolutely not."

"Good, then get up here so I can suck that gorgeous cock of yours. I want to show you how much you please me."

Trax's eyes flared wide, and I sensed his mixture of relief, male satisfaction and arousal.

"As you see, I've got tons of scars. They show we've lived, that we've survived. They're like… badges of honor." I used the word *honor* because it seemed they were full of it, that maybe he'd understand then. "Are you repulsed by me and my marks?"

I felt anger. "Far from it."

"The same goes for me. Surnen's cock needs to be put to use."

"Hurry, fucker. She's hot, wet and tight, and you're talking about your feelings."

That pushed Trax into action. He walked around to the bottom of the bed, then crawled up so he knelt just beyond Surnen's head.

"Very well, mate. Every hole filled," Trax commented, his fist working its way up and down the huge length.

I licked my lips when another pearly drop appeared. I leaned forward, set my hands on his muscled thighs and licked it. He gripped himself still, held it out for me.

The musky flavor hit my tongue, and I went at him like an ice cream cone that needed to be eaten before it melted in the sun. I could get him into my mouth, but I was stretched wide. If he expected deep throating, it wasn't going to happen.

The butt plug began to vibrate then, and I moaned around his cock.

Trax kept his hand at the base of himself, but his free hand cupped my cheek, then tangled in my hair. "Hot and wet," he growled, his concerns completely forgotten in a haze of desire.

Surnen thrust his hips up and agreed. "Hot and wet everywhere."

They moved then, fucking me in cautious yet thorough motions, as if learning me. Learning what made me feel good, and they could sense it through the sounds I made around Trax's cock and the collar.

I might have been on top, but Surnen had all the control. That was fine with me, for he knew just how to wield that beast between his legs. He rubbed over spots I hadn't even known were hot. And the plug... the combination was ruthless to my control. I had none.

The baseness of having a cock in my mouth too, completely filled by my mates, pushed me to the brink, then over. I screamed my pleasure, but the sound was muffled by Trax's thick length. They didn't take long to follow me over, but the rush, the pulse of their orgasms merging with mine through the collars was like the most intense aftershock ever.

Trax's cum burst onto my tongue, and I swallowed it greedily. Surnen held my hips in the tightest of grips keeping himself deep.

"Mikki," he growled as he pumped his seed into me.

Trax backed up, and I popped off him and tried to catch my breath, the flavor of him on my tongue. It was too much, too intense. I dropped onto Surnen's chest, and his arms went around me. He was still hard deep inside me, as if he'd never come. The plug stopped vibrating, going quiet, although the nerves there were still firing and keeping me aroused.

"Mmm, mate. You are not satisfied," he said finally. His skin was hot to the touch, and we were both slick with sweat. Trax's hand stroked down my back, and I knew he was right there with us.

"I am sooo satisfied," I replied.

"But you are not done," he said.

I lifted my head and rested my chin on my hand. "And you are? It doesn't feel like it."

I clenched my inner walls, and seed seeped out.

"Mate," he growled.

"It's Trax's turn." I looked up at him. I couldn't miss the satisfied smile on his face, the way his dark cock was still ruthlessly hard.

He shook his head. "Your pussy is for your primary male."

I frowned, glanced back at Surnen. He nodded.

"What?"

"You will be bred by your primary male," he explained. "Only then can a second's cock be sated there."

I sat up and gasped as Surnen went deeper, but carefully lifted up and off his cock. A gush of seed slipped from me and landed on his stomach.

"Fuck, that is hot," he commented.

I rolled my eyes. "I want Trax, too."

"Mate," Surnen warned. "That is not the way things are done."

"The one thing you can't command is my uterus, *mate.*

My uterus says no to breeding. No babies anytime soon. You can just let Trax get in there and have some fun."

Trax was biting his lip to keep from smiling. Surnen pushed up onto his elbows to look at me.

"You raise a valid point," he stated.

My mouth fell open. "Really?"

"Yes. It is your choice if you do not wish for children now. While I desire them, the idea of not sharing you with anyone but Trax for the near term is pleasing to me." He reached up, rubbed his thumb over one of my nipples, then leaned forward and laved it with his tongue, with a gentleness that belied his harsh rules, his stern demeanor. There was a sensitive side to him as well. "I am a greedy man. I do not wish to share these with an infant."

My nipple went instantly hard. "That's... that's good."

"Denying Trax the pleasure of that perfect pussy would be cruel."

"Exactly."

Surnen sat up, looked to Trax and nodded.

Trax didn't wait a second, just hooked me about the waist, lifted me and tossed me onto the bed. I was on my back, and he was above me, pressing me down from one heartbeat to the next. His cock pressed into my thigh. I ran my finger over his integrations, studied them, but I wasn't bothered. I tried to push those feelings to him through the collar so he'd be reassured. He smiled down at me as if he'd picked it up, quite pleased with himself. And aroused. His worries gone.

"What about the plug?" I asked, running a finger along his jaw.

"What about it?" he asked.

"Can it come out now?" I didn't mind it. In fact, it made

me wetter, which was impossible since I was practically dripping with Surnen's seed.

"No," Surnen said from beside the bed. "It stays in. I shall bring you some food, mate."

Trax shifted his hips and thrust into me in one long strong stroke. He growled. I moaned.

"You're going to need it."

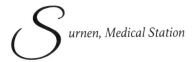

urnen, Medical Station

"You've been sucking face for five minutes. Either get a room or get out," Rachel barked. She looked my way and rolled her eyes. I'd seen her do it before when her mates' backs were turned, and I recognized it as a human's sign of bother.

I stifled a smile at the way Trax was struggling to take his mouth and hands off our mate. They were in the entry of the medical lab, preventing the door from closing. Rachel had been here when we arrived, busy with her latest task. She was a proven scientist and a valuable member of the medical group.

Mikki whimpered and her fingers were clutching at Trax's uniform shirt. I was hard, not only from watching them but from the blast of arousal—like an ion cannon— they sent my way through the collars.

We'd taken her first thing this morning, but I understood Trax's hesitancy to separate. I hadn't been aware of the depth and extent of his insecurities about his integrations. Many on The Colony had pride issues, were vain to a certain degree, about how their bodies had changed at the hands of the Hive. I saw it as survival, and so had Mikki, based on what she'd told Trax the night before. His concerns were in his head and only valid with her. She was the one who could make them an issue, who could destroy him in a second if she displayed fear or horror at seeing the silver.

It had been a good thing I'd bared myself to her in the transport room. She'd seen my integrations first. Knew what they looked like, knew what to expect when Trax had bared himself. She hadn't been repulsed by me, so Trax's fears were unfounded.

Satisfaction in Mikki was overwhelming. She'd eased Trax's concerns within seconds, shutting him down by sharing her own marks. Fuck, Earth was primitive. Her skin was marred, and I hated to know she'd suffered. But perhaps they were there to prove to Trax that everyone was broken in some way.

The way her tongue was down his throat, it seemed he'd gotten over his issues readily enough. Now he wouldn't stop touching her.

She was ours, and work was an annoyance. Our cocks ruled us. I didn't dare believe we'd surrendered too much power to Mikki. Not yet.

"Seriously," Rachel added. The beeps and sounds of the lab were lulling to me, but hopefully for Trax it was a reminder that he wasn't in our bedroom. While I didn't mind watching them together, the idea of someone walking by and seeing Mikki's passion, hearing her sounds of pleasure made me ready to fight anyone in the pit who witnessed it.

Trax lifted his head and gave Rachel a glare, although it was somewhat muted by his lust for Mikki. He sighed and rubbed his thumb over Mikki's lower lip. "Fine," he said, giving her ass a light swat to push her away from him, but he didn't go far.

"Hey!" she protested.

I settled into my work, content to have Mikki nearby. We'd yet to discuss what she would do here... other than pleasure us sexually.

Perhaps it was the environment, but my mind turned to my work. I was creating the final steps in the treatment process and was going to add it to the ReGen pod to test on the healing warriors. I'd brought my supplies and had added the serum I'd watched kill the bacteria the day before —just prior to Mikki's arrival—although there was nothing to do now since the pods did all the work.

Claiming my new mate had been paramount and had prolonged the effects of the few Prillon warriors infected with the virus, but I had no regrets. Now I was content. My collar was around her neck. My seed was inside her body, not growing into a child—not yet—but there was time. I had all the time in the world now that Mikki was mine. I would not let her go at the end of our thirty days, of that I was certain. However, I had a feeling she had not yet accepted that as truth.

Trax's job was part of a patrol unit, monitoring the underground caves and other places we had discovered the Hive liked to hide. We hadn't had an incident in some time, but they were relentless. So were we.

He would be doubly diligent now. Like me, he had something precious to protect.

Mikki.

I wanted to ensure the serum was working, then we would take her on a tour of Base 3, but she understood the sick warriors took priority.

"How long do they have to stay in there?" she asked, running her small hand along the outside of a ReGen pod, this one and the next occupied by Prillon warriors who were now recovering. The serum was working. I had promised Prime Nial a cure, and I had delivered on that promise, as always. Now to be patient while the remaining sick were healed; then I could share it with the Fleet. This illness would be a thing of the past.

"A few more hours, mate. Then they will be free to go."

"This is so amazing." The awe in her voice pleased me. Not much impressed my mate, and even that facet of her personality I found endearing. She was cynical and questioned everything. She was, in many ways, much like me.

"The ReGen technology is several centuries old, but every living thing fights for survival, even the smallest virus. Sometimes what we can't see does the most damage."

"It's the same on Earth," she replied. "Hundreds... hell, millions of people have died of an outbreak. Why don't we have these pod things? We are part of the Coalition now, right? Why didn't you guys give this technology to Earth?" Her tone of voice was pleasant, innocent, but we were connected by the collars and I clearly felt the anger simmering beneath. Why should humans suffer and die if it was preventable?

"Because the technology can be used to kill as well as

heal, and Earth is a provisional member of the Coalition of Planets, not a full member. The very first human matched in the Interstellar Brides Program was tasked with stealing our technology to send back to your human government. Luckily her mates discovered her plan before it was too late."

"What?" She glanced from me to Rachel, who sat working nearby, staring into the odd contraption she had created with the S-Gen machine upon her arrival. She called it a microscope. I had, at first, thought it nonsense. Everything she did could be done more easily with the microviewer and screen used by every doctor in the Fleet. But she had won me over, and I now often preferred to work on the odd contraption when she was not in the lab. Had even considered creating one of my own.

Rachel must have felt her gaze, for she responded even before lifting her head. "It's true, Mikki. She was CIA. First bride ever sent out into space. They thought the Coalition made up the whole thing. The Hive. The danger. Everything, just to gain control of Earth."

Mikki sputtered. "That's stupid."

"Agreed." Rachel finally looked up and smiled. "So, what exactly does a professional surfer do anyway? Well, besides surf."

There were politics between Earth and the Coalition. Mikki was too new to understand both perspectives, and I was relieved Rachel changed the subject.

The surge of Mikki's happiness at the question shocked me, and I realized I'd been an ass. I had no idea what a professional surfer was, but it was obviously something rewarding and fulfilling for my mate. Trax had asked her what she'd done for a job the night before, but I'd been balls-deep in her pussy and forgotten all about it.

I stilled, waited.

"Actually I'm an environmental scientist. I was working as a contractor for the EPA as an environmental monitor. I specialized in environmental cleanup. That's before I was arrested, of course."

"What is this EPA?" I asked.

"Environmental Protection Agency. A branch of our government."

I nodded in understanding and she continued.

"I haven't surfed for more than fun since I was twenty-two. Back then, I traveled the world. Scuba dived every chance I got. It was awesome to be so young and carefree. God, it was great while it lasted."

"While it lasted?" Rachel asked, a frown forming on her brow. She usually had it when she was confused by what she was seeing in her microscope. "What happened?"

I leaned forward, interested.

Mikki tucked her sleek hair behind her ear. "I was in Australia for a tournament. A big wave rolled me, and I hit a reef. Had a severe concussion and facial fracture. I would have continued to compete, but it was my third concussion and my father, who is a doctor, basically threatened me with bodily harm and made me watch Internet videos of Muhammad Ali and a bunch of other athletes who could barely function because of past head trauma. You know, CTE."

Rachel nodded in understanding of the gibberish. I could not understand a word of it, but I sensed through the collar her lingering frustration and disappointment.

"What is this Internet?" Trax asked.

Rachel answered. "It's like the comm system the Fleet uses. All of Earth's data is stored and accessed via the Internet."

"And what is CTE?"

Mikki shrugged helplessly. "A brain disease?"

Brain disease? Mikki was unwell? I stood, my chair scraping across the floor. "Trax, get me my scanner. Get a tech to ready a pod. I knew you needed a medical exam."

Rachel held up a hand, stopping Trax. "Cool your jets," she said. "It's called Chronic Trauma Encephalopathy. Humans who have repeated head injuries can develop a degenerative condition that leads to impaired brain function and dementia."

"That is not making me feel any better," I snapped.

If this CTE was something that Mikki's father feared would affect her, I would study the disease and make sure nothing would ever happen to my female. And put her in a ReGen pod immediately to heal her.

Anxiety. Discomfort. My mate's emotions bombarded me as Rachel discussed this strange human condition. I would not upset her this way, not when I now had what was necessary to research my mate's medical condition on my own.

"I don't *have* CTE, Surnen," Mikki said. "He was just afraid I could get it if I kept competing."

"Come here, mate."

I gave a command, and I expected it to be obeyed. Mikki walked to me slowly, but irritation and—*embarrassment*—were clearly conveyed to me through our collars.

How did such a small, delicate creature have so many, and such violent, emotions in the span of a few minutes? Nothing she felt was moderated. Every emotion through the collars was like an explosion inside my mind, unsettling me. Personally I avoided feeling this much, this intensely. There was no need. Such emotion was a handicap when facing crisis or managing the many serious duties I had. I would speak to her about this later, when we were alone. She would learn more control.

Lifting my hands to gently cup her face, I was appeased when Rachel's attention returned to her work, her gaze once again upon what she saw through her microscope. Mikki was so small, her skin so soft. I wanted to hold her, keep her safe from even her past. "Explain this... surfing. If you could get a disease from it, why did you do it?"

Mikki sighed, but I felt her emotions swell right before she spoke. "I know you have water here, for I've used the shower tube. Drank it. I don't know if there are any oceans on the planet."

"There aren't," Rachel said.

Mikki bit her lip. "Yeah, well. Imagine water for as far as you can see. Nothing but water."

I frowned, thought about the idea.

"Here," Rachel said, pulling up an image on the comm screen. I released my hold on Mikki, but she didn't move other than to look up, then smile. I felt a calmness settle over her, which soothed me.

Trax turned to look at the screen and crossed his arms over his chest.

The image was of water, all dark blue with ripples across the surface, then light blue sky. The image changed and changed again of this water. So much of it. So many different colors of blue, green and gray tipped with white. Fascinating.

"Those are waves. They crash on the edge of land. For

fun, people ride them, and that's called surfing." Mikki waited a moment as Rachel pulled up an image of a small human riding a pointed slat across the surface of the water. "Yes, like that."

Rachel was able to program the machine to have images change in and out. From water the color of the brightest blue to almost black. Wild and tempestuous, calm and serene. Then these waves, some two or three times as tall as the humans on boards, attempting to remain standing.

"Insanity," I murmured, now understanding. I sensed her happiness at the images, the longing, the appreciation. It *was* beautiful but so foreign to me. Yet it made me understand my mate, a place deep inside her.

Mikki laughed. She was pleased.

"Are there any images of you?" I asked.

The screen went blank and Mikki appeared. From a distance it was hard to tell it was her, but I was her mate. I *knew* her.

"Gods," I said, transfixed. "What the fuck are you wearing where humans could see you?"

She surfed beautifully in tiny scraps of cloth covering her breasts and pussy. I now knew how she gained the... tan lines as she called them. From what I could tell, then there was a video of her falling, of a massive wall of water collapsing on top of her.

"Mate," I growled, feeling instantly afraid. I knew she'd survived since she was standing before me, but still... "Enough!" I snapped. I might understand her, but I didn't like her reckless nature. It scared the shit out of me.

Rachel quickly turned off the comm screen.

"Sooooo, that's surfing," Mikki commented. "And waves. And the ocean."

"It is beautiful," Trax said, turning to look at Mikki. "I might be Prillon, but I was born on a battleship. Raised on one. The first time I touched a planet was at the Academy, and only for a short time. Then I was back in space except during battle. Being here, it is the longest I have been on ground." Trax shook his head. "How can I be a good mate if I do not even understand what it is like to be... one with your planet?"

I sensed his concerns. I'd been raised on Prillon Prime. I didn't have allegiance to the place, but I knew what ground felt like. Water, although nothing like what I'd just seen. Trees. Animals. Trax didn't.

"A perfect match doesn't mean we have to be alike. The best relationships are often founded on being opposites," Mikki told him.

"Yeah, look at me and Maxim," Rachel offered, giving Trax an understanding smile. "I tolerate him."

I bit my lip. "I shall be sure to tell him that."

Rachel's eyes widened. "Yeah, no."

"I would not know what to do with all that water," Trax added, although I sensed he was calmed by the females' words. "And on such a small piece of wood."

"You aren't the only one," Rachel told him. "And I'm from Earth. Don't worry, Trax. Even Earth guys couldn't compete with that."

Mikki shrugged. "They could if they practiced."

"And that would make you want them more than you wanted to get back on the board?" Rachel asked.

Mikki blushed and I felt something strange through the collar. Longing? Sadness? Regret, perhaps. Did she miss the ocean so much? Was she not going to be happy here with me? With Trax?

I gave her a nod, for she was thorough, or at least Rachel
was in her imagery. It helped quite a bit, even though it had
made Trax panic. "I appreciate your desire, your drive to
surf. I think I'd rather fight a Hive trio than one of those
waves on a board," I admitted. "I admire your fearlessness,
but you did not inform me that you had been injured."

"It was a long time ago."

That was not the answer I wished to hear.

"You refused to submit to a medical exam, and I allowed
it. You will tell me now. I need to know every single injury
and lingering weakness so that I may assess your health and
properly care for you."

"I'm fine." She turned her head in an attempt to break
away, but I held fast. Dominant. Demanding. She was mine.
She would obey.

"You will catalog your injuries and defects to me so that I
may treat you and assure your health. Now, or you shall be
in an exam room, stripped and analyzed."

"For once, I agree with Surnen," Trax said, stepping
closer and crossing his arms over his chest.

She looked between us. "Holy crap on a cracker. Are you
kidding me with this?"

Rachel chuckled and that small sound broke the tension
from Mikki's body. "They aren't kidding. Get used to it,
Earth girl. You aren't in Kansas anymore."

"Fine," she grumbled. "I broke my middle toe
kicking a soccer ball in sixth grade. I've had stitches all
over my body from catching the fin on my board or
rolling under and hitting rocks or coral. Coral is, well...
an animal, but it looks like rock and it's often hard. It's
under the water and is what makes waves... partly." She
sighed because I sensed her difficulty in explaining

something I'd never seen. "I've had three concussions, all fine now, and I broke the bones around my left eye. I have wires holding my cheekbone together on the left side, but they buried the scars behind my hairline so no one would see them. I blew my ACL—" At my look, she clarified. "The ligament in my left knee, had it rebuilt... *human* style, and then tore it again. So two surgeries there."

"Stop." I could not take any more of this, especially knowing there had been no ReGen wand or pod nearby to help her. It was a wonder she was alive. "You will not abuse your body this way. Voluntarily going into the dangerous water... on a small board. Do you understand?" Mikki had more injuries than some fighters I knew.

"Now you do sound like my father," she snapped.

"Then he was a highly intelligent male."

She frowned, practically scowled. "That is true. But I don't recommend talking to me the way he did."

"Why not? He sounds like a good father."

She pulled away, her eyes closed tightly. Her snort was rude, but it was the pain coming through the collar that made me let her go this time.

"Textbook."

Again I was lost. "Rachel? Please translate this term."

Rachel spun in her chair, leaned back and looked at me, and the pity in her eyes made me anxious, as it was not for Mikki but for me. "Textbook, on Earth, implies that the thing being discussed is perfect on paper. Every rule followed. Everything that is socially expected and considered normal has been done. So her father was, in the eyes of the world, perfect."

I turned to my mate. "I do not understand. If your father

was perfect, why do I feel such pain and buried anger coming from you when you speak of him?"

Mikki reached up and tugged at her collar as if it pained her. As if the connection we shared was a burden.

Rachel chuckled again. "Can't hide anything out here, Mik. And they are relentless."

"You would know," Mikki fired back at her new friend.

"Exactly."

What were these human females discussing? And why had Rachel referred to my mate as Mik? That was not her name. "My mate's name is Mikki," I stated.

"Of course, it is." Rachel's smile was unreadable.

Females.

"I wish to scan your body to assess the lingering effects of these injuries."

Mikki shook her head. "Oh no. I know you think humans live like Neanderthals and our healing methods are primitive." She glanced at the line of pods. "Which they probably are, but I'm fine."

"Surnen," Rachel began. "I'm impressed you didn't give your mate an exam." She gave me a pointed look that told me she had yet to forget her own. "However, if you wish to get lucky ever again, you may just want to limit your obsession to a simple body scan."

"Get lucky?" I asked, confused.

"Sex," Mikki added, eyeing me. "If you ever want to have sex with me, ever again, you won't even think about coming at me with your alien probes."

Rachel snorted and I narrowed my gaze at her. Those probes saved lives, and if my mate needed assistance—

"I mean it. If Rachel is not freaking over this body scan, then I'll allow that. Nothing more."

Trax handed a wand to me. I hadn't seen him grab it, but I was thankful and began to slowly move it in front of her body. She rolled her eyes but stood still to allow it. As if she had a choice.

Within thirty seconds the review was done and she was well. The scan didn't reveal any defect, especially this CTE, but it did catalog prior injuries and scars. The ReGen pods didn't heal old wounds, only fresh ones. Unless I wanted to take Mikki into surgery, reopen old wounds or rebreak old bones, then there was no point. Sometimes, such extreme measures were required, but I could not willingly damage my female. If she required such treatment, I would need to call in another doctor to inflict the injuries to her body.

And they would have to lock me in a prison cell while they hurt her, or I would most likely kill them.

"Relax, Surnen. Seriously I'm fine." Mikki's hand ran up and down my forearm in an attempt to comfort me, and I realized I'd allowed my extreme thoughts to bleed through the collar to her.

"I am fine, as is our mate. She does not have this CTE they spoke of." I nodded and Trax relaxed as I focused on changing the tone of my thoughts. "There are some probes you might enjoy, mate," I advised, and I took pleasure in her cheeks turning pink.

Trax and I had certainly tested her health and fitness since we'd fucked her into exhaustion. I knew every inch of her body. If she had an ache, it was because we'd fucked her too hard. If she had a pain, it was because I'd tugged on her nipples to the point where her discomfort morphed into pleasure.

No, the scans were clear, but I would carry the health

scanner on my uniform, just in case. Dropping my hand, I gave her a nod, and she stepped away.

Mikki went to Rachel's side, and the governor's mate was kind and friendly toward her as she explained the project she was working on. We had received information from a Coalition exobiology team that something was causing a strange disease to develop in a native animal species on Valuri.

The Fleet did not have time to investigate such matters, and as Valuri was relatively close to The Colony, I had agreed to look over their data. Animals weren't my specialty, especially on a planet not my own. Rachel, a worthy scientist in her own right, had taken over the task when the first two Prillon warriors became ill. I'd shifted my focus to finding a cure for them while she studied Valuri's problems.

"Is that the planet you're helping?" Mikki asked.

I glanced over my shoulder to see vivid images of Valuri on the comm screen on the wall opposite Rachel. The planet was a chaotic mess of life. The orange star hovering in the sky above the landscape covered a large part of the sky. The cooler star emitted reddish light, which cause the ocean to have a brownish-red hue that was unlike the blue water vids I had seen of Earth. Still, Mikki stared, fascinated.

"Is that a lake or is that their ocean?"

With the images that Rachel had shared of Earth's water, I now saw similarities. The planets were near each other, at least in universe metrics. "Ocean. But there is no *they*. The planet is uninhabited. At least by people."

"You said animals are getting sick? Are they carbon based or something extreme, like sulfur?"

"Carbon, we assume." Rachel answered her. "The

planet's environment is very similar to Earth's, as a matter of fact. Nearly identical."

"Even the atmosphere?"

"Again, nearly identical, although Valuri appears to have higher oxygen levels than Earth as well as a thicker cover of ozone in the higher atmosphere protecting the surface from ultraviolet radiation. With their star so close to the planet, they probably need the extra protection."

"What kind of animals are getting sick? Land or sea?"

"Coalition satellites spotted group beachings of dead sea creatures about the size of Earth's orcas. The smallest group they saw was seven, the largest close to thirty. They beach, then after a day or two the carcasses disappear. We figure they are being scavenged by local wildlife."

"Are they mammals?"

"We don't know. No one's been there yet. The Coalition sent probes, but they gathered general data. Nothing specific about the animals on the planet. With the war going on, and no known civilization living there, exploring wasn't a high priority."

"So they sent it to you?"

"To us," I confirmed. "One of the things we do here is investigate things the battleships do not have time to invest in."

"Because you are sent here to die, and you have all the time in the world. Is that it?" Mikki's anger simmered again, but I did not understand the reason behind it. She spoke truth.

"Yes. I work on things the doctors in the Fleet do not have time to investigate. As does Rachel. We are an asset to the Coalition, despite our diminished status as citizens on The Colony."

"Don't even get me started, Surnen." Mikki waved her hand at me to indicate I should stop speaking and returned her attention to Rachel, who was looking up at my mate with a strange expression on her face. One I'd never seen before.

"I know, right? It's ridiculous the way they treat their veterans."

"This place is insane."

"Yeah, well, before Jessica was matched to Prime Nial, these guys couldn't even get brides."

"That's bullshit." Mikki looked at me then, her gaze meeting mine, and I felt despair coming from her. Sadness. And rage.

"I know."

I could not feel Rachel's emotions, but the two human women had nearly identical facial expressions. If Rachel felt as Mikki did, I wondered that I did not see Maxim or Ryston walking into the medical lab. Perhaps they had grown accustomed to a human female's wild emotional swings. One moment Mikki was in awe, feeling wonder and excitement, the next arousal, then rage followed by despair. My mind could not adapt so quickly.

"Let's change the subject before I get myself in trouble. So, the creatures are washing up in groups, running in pods?" Mikki asked.

"Again, that's the theory."

"So, they're social. Could be intelligent." Mikki's gaze was tipped up at the screen. "Okay. So, the planet has a dwarf star, orange or red, not as hot as our sun. I understand the red coloring of the water, but why does the water look so thick and muddy? Is that some kind of fungal bloom? I would be concerned about oxygen and nitrogen levels in the water, especially close to shore. That could be affecting the animals. They could be suffocating."

Rachel glanced up at her. "A surfer and now an exobiologist?"

Mikki shook her head. "I wouldn't go that far. But I do know the ocean. As I said, environmental testing is my specialty. I worked for a private contractor that analyzed water samples for contamination and oversaw cleanup. I was part of the emergency response crews, specifically in Hawaii and along the West Coast. Oil spills, military pollutants, manufacturing emissions, sewer waste. We specialized in using bacteria and other natural solutions to clean up whatever mess we were sent to. In my free time I spearheaded the save-the-planet campaigns, like the whale ship fiasco that got me put in jail."

"Impressive," Rachel commented, then looked toward me and Trax. "Besides having brass balls, your mate is a scientist like us, Surnen. She'll be an asset here. Might even need to hire her for this project because I'm a lab rat, a biochemist, but she knows environment science and ecology." She cocked her head toward the image of Vulari's ocean on the comm screen. "And that is so not my specialty."

I didn't know what brass balls were, and Rachel was clearly not a rodent, but I understood her meaning. My mate was very brave. And she knew a lot about natural systems, living systems. Of which The Colony had almost none. We were primarily a mining planet. The few scraggly shrubs that managed to cling to some kind of life in the soil were adapted to the harsh conditions found outside Base 3's containment fields. There would be nothing for my mate to study here. Nothing to occupy her brilliant mind. And that would be a problem, would lead to Mikki becoming unhappy.

"If the water is as polluted as it appears, I'd love to help clean it up. That's my jam."

Rachel laughed. "We know."

I cut in. "The water isn't polluted. Valuri's dwarf star does not emit white light in the same spectrum as your sun, mate." I *had* studied much of Earth after the first human brides had begun to arrive.

"I understand that. But despite the color of that star, that water does not look right. Trust me. I've spent years of my life in the water, and that water isn't just red. There's something wrong there." Her words rang true as curiosity and awe moved through the collars. So volatile, my mate. I was not going to be able to work this way. Her presence completely wrecked my concentration. I wasn't Everian, but I could practically scent her. I knew she had my cum— Trax's, too— deep inside her pussy. I still had the flavor of her on my tongue. My fingers tingled with the remembrance of her silky skin. My cock stirred remembering the tight clench of her inner walls as I made her scream.

I could not think straight with her in my presence. Neither would I be able to concentrate if she were elsewhere, for then I would wonder if she was well. Fuck, I was in trouble.

"A crew is heading over there in a few hours. You should come with us because we could really use your help."

"Over... you mean you're going to Valuri? Really?" Rachel nodded.

"Yes!" Mikki practically clapped her hands with glee.

"No," Trax and I said at the same time. Our responses were immediate.

My female was not leaving The Colony. I couldn't handle allowing her out of the room, let alone off planet. "It's not safe."

"Oh, give me a break, Surnen," Rachel said. "You can't keep her locked up here. I know who she worked for, the company's reputation. She could help us. Clearly she knows about water, about contamination. We could use her expertise and a fresh perspective." Rachel's words caused my mate to cross her arms and scowl at me in agreement. I was used to her naked, unused to her in the pants she wore with a long, flowing top. The soft material was cream colored but would soon be gray to match the color of her collar.

"I don't doubt her abilities," I replied and Trax nodded. "We have only recently learned of her extensive list of prior injuries. She could get hurt."

"I'm not a child. I made it here all the way from Earth, didn't I?" Simmering rage. That's what was pinging me now, like needles in my mind as my mate's ire grew. "I'm not a prisoner. Not anymore. I can probably help this planet and those poor sea creatures that are dying. I can't just let them die without trying to help. It's not my way."

The longing in her voice nearly broke me, but it was Rachel's next words that won Mikki her heart's desire.

"She is your mate," Rachel said, looking to both of us. "She must live her life, be useful here. Maxim and Ryston understood that, and you have to admit I'm useful."

"You saved us all, Lady Rone." I bowed to her now, not in mockery but out of respect. When Maxim had been reactivated by Hive frequencies being broadcast within medical, she had been the one to figure out what was going on. She had solved the puzzle and helped us unmask the traitor, Krael. Captain Brooks had died, but she had saved Maxim's life, and the rest of us by proxy. Without her, the Hive would have invaded The Colony and reactivated each and every one of us. Used us in their war. Forced us to kill our friends and our allies.

She was a smart woman, knew exactly what she was doing. I couldn't deny she'd been instrumental in saving lives. But this wasn't just any life we were talking about. This was Mikki. My mate. My life. My heart and hope and future. Already she was everything.

"You can't deny, as a scientist, that we need her skill set for this project. The timing of her arrival couldn't be better. I spent my working life in a pharmaceutical lab, not out in the field. You have to let her go with the crew today."

Then she said the one sentence that I couldn't deny.

"I need her help." Rachel stood and placed a hand on Mikki's shoulder. "I need her brain. Seriously, Surnen. We need her in the field."

I sighed, looked to Trax. I felt his concern but also his understanding. We were going to have to let Mikki out of our sight. I just hadn't expected it to be so soon after her arrival.

"You know I'm going with a crew of six," Rachel said to me. "Maxim and Ryston are just as nuts as you are about security. Six armed guards on an uninhabited planet. All we'll be doing is taking samples and doing some analysis."

Six armed guards. The thought made me smile. Of course. The governor and his second would not allow their treasured female to be in danger. "I am not some kind of tree seed, and neither are your mates," I countered. "But I concede your point. If Mikki can help with the project, she must go."

Mikki's smile made my heart leap. I had pleased her, which pleased me. But I instantly thought of my parents. The loss. This wasn't the same. I wasn't giving up rules and protocols to please my mate. She was going with a dedicated crew on a scientific mission. Protocols were in place. She would be with Rachel, who I was satisfied would *never* be unprotected. Not as the governor's mate.

Rachel stood. "Let's get the hell out of Dodge before Surly over there changes his mind."

"Mate," I called. Mikki stopped, turned to face me and Trax.

"I shall allow you to go."

"Allow?" she countered, tapping her foot.

"Allow," I repeated. "Rachel, she will catch up with you at transport."

The human must have understood we wanted privacy, for she picked up her things and left, the door sliding closed behind her.

"Now, mate. You may go to Valuri, but I must have you first. My cock is hard and needs sating."

Heat flared through the collars. Trax went to work on her pants, quickly opened them and worked them over her hips.

"Is this protocol? Fucking your mate before she heads off to work?" she asked.

I grinned. She wasn't averse to what we were about to do. In fact, when Trax lifted her up and set her upon my workbench, removing her pants the rest of the way so she was bare to us, she didn't resist. She helped by toeing off her shoes and letting them fall to the floor.

Opening my own pants and gripping my cock, stroking it, I stalked toward her. "Mate protocol 2.467a."

Her eyes widened. "Seriously?"

"Yes." I dropped to my knees before her, pushed her thighs wide. "Part A is eating a mate's pussy until she screams her release." Leaning in, I kissed my way up her thigh toward her center. I scented her arousal, saw it. Her juices, our cum still on her.

"Protocol 2.467b is fucking her until she forgets her name," Trax added. "Both of us."

There was no such thing as protocol 2.467, a or b, but she didn't know that. When I put my mouth on her, she didn't care either, tangling her fingers in my hair. It seemed we'd found some rules she wouldn't fight.

9

*M*ikki, *Planet Valuri, The Beach*

THE TWISTING TORMENT of the transporting to another world left me doubled over, gasping for air.

"That stinks," I complained to Rachel, who stood next to me in a similar condition. She smacked me on the shoulder through the thick protection of the space suit I was wearing and grinned.

"Never get used to it, but it beats spending ten hours cramped in coach on an airplane back home."

"True." I stood and looked out over the new horizon of an alien world and forgot that two seconds ago I'd felt like I was dying, my chest squeezed and my head pounding as if it was about to explode. "Wow."

"Right?" Rachel was already moving toward the water, directing one of the six large warriors to position her lab and sampling equipment that had transported with us.

Everyone but Rachel was covered head to toe in the same black and gray space suit with cool, *Star Trek* inspired helmets. Since Rachel was with medical, her suit was dark green. Rachel had said this was their first visit to the planet, even though they'd been monitoring and testing for weeks. The data had come back that the planet was habitable, meaning the oxygen levels could sustain life—thus, the plants and greenery I could see beyond the beach.

Protocol—Surnen wasn't the only one who followed the rules—dictated we wear full life support until a crew could confirm we wouldn't drop dead from some random gas or imbalance. I was used to being in a bikini on a beach, not covered from head to toe.

It was midday, a small reddish-orange disk hovering directly overhead. I couldn't gauge the temperature, not with the space suit on, but it looked pleasant. To be perfectly honest, I wasn't sure what a nice day looked like in this place, but to me, it was beautiful. Coral, rose and soft yellows filled the sky, making the clouds glow like cotton candy. The sky wasn't blue, not like Earth, but the color I'd only ever seen just before the sun rose, when the sky was more pink than blue.

Through the space helmet, I glanced down at the sand, for it was the thick, movable stuff that made my feet sink with every step. Joy rippled through me, and I was shocked to feel tears streaking down my face as longing for this—the water, the sand, the open sky—welled up in me like a tsunami of emotion. I thought I'd made peace with never seeing the ocean again.

I'd been wrong. So, so wrong. Grief at the loss felt like a dormant volcano suddenly about to erupt.

"Mate, are you well?" Surnen's voice came through my

comms, and I shrugged off the melancholy swamping me. I was familiar with the deep-water masks from scuba, but they'd never had communications built in. Hearing someone clearly, as if they were right next to me instead of on a different planet, was cool but unfamiliar.

He must have felt my pain through the collars. Damn things. Was this my life now? The men in my bed knowing everything I felt, even when I was on another planet? My pussy still ached, though, a reminder of how much I liked his bossiness, of the rules he had. Some of them, I liked. No, loved. I was *never* going to forget protocol 2.467a *or* b.

"Answer me, Mikki." His stern tone was a reminder that I had new adventures ahead of me, with or without the ocean. I would simply have to learn to love rocks. I could do that. Right?

"I'm fine," I replied. "I guess I was passed out when I transported from Earth. I'm not used to the feel. God, it's like using a portkey in *Harry Potter.*"

"You have transport on Earth?" Surnen asked. I couldn't miss the surprise in his voice.

I laughed. "No. A woman wrote a book about something like it. Never mind."

"I feel your pain, mate," he replied, his voice sharp with his familiar sternness. "It is faint, but I feel it nonetheless. Perhaps you should return to The Colony."

"We just got here. I'm fine." His suggestion that I transport back effectively buried every other emotion beneath anger. I was not going to return just because this place, even at first glimpse, reminded me of Earth, of what I would miss on The Colony's barren terrain. Not happening. "If you can't handle it, just take your collar off, Surnen. I have emotions. I feel things. I'll let you know if I need you."

A sharp sting hit me through the collar, and I realized I had hurt him. Damn it. I didn't want that either.

I sighed. "I'm sorry, Surnen. Mate. Please, I'm all right." I looked around, took in the expanse of reddish water all the way to the horizon on my right, lush foliage with a mix of shrubbery and trees meeting the edge of the beach. I felt like I'd been shipwrecked on a deserted island.

"There are six huge warriors working on the beach. They'll protect me, and there's not another soul in sight. Rachel is setting up the equipment. Thank you for checking on me, but I'm exactly where I need to be right now."

"Are you sure?" Surnen asked warily.

"You have your work conquering sickness. This is what I do. What I'm good at. I *need* to be useful."

I heard him growl, and it made me laugh. "More useful than in your bed."

"Yes, mate. You are quite useful there." I felt the blast of arousal through the collar, and I squirmed, rubbing my thighs together to ease the sudden ache.

His silence stretched, but the sting coming from him had faded when I used the word *mate.* "Very well, but you will follow protocol to the letter. Do not remove your helmet and do not take any unnecessary risks. I will not see you hurt."

Well, he was bossy and protective and kind of adorable in his gruff way. What a worrier. Sheesh. Maybe it was a doctor thing, always expecting the worst.

"I won't."

"I will monitor your progress as I am able."

"Of course you will."

"Mate, continue to defy me and you will be over my knee upon your return."

That made me hot. "You promise?" With that teasing

remark—and, I was sure, my desire for exactly that kind of play winging across the stars to him through whatever miracle of quantum physics made these collars work over long distances—I ended the comm and walked over to Rachel. "So, tell me what we've got."

She was shoving sample collection rods into the sand along the edge of the surf. The waves here were small, perhaps only two or three feet tall. As I scanned the water, I had to assume there was no coral or offshore drop-off to form larger waves.

"Well, we've got new data since we last spoke. The Coalition telescopes picked up an anomaly in the atmospheric temperature here. Rapid changes for no apparent reason. The planet has been warming, the clouds are thinning, and AI analysis shows a dangerous decline in the planet's ability to support life if the trend continues."

I pointed to the wall of bright, brilliant flowers and foliage lining one cliff face. "Clearly this issue hasn't been going on for long. The plant life is still thriving." I inspected the water, what I could see of it. "And I don't see any abnormal blooms in the water here."

She turned her head. "Right. No dead animal carcasses either. We need to figure out what's going on before the shift endangers all life on the planet. I don't want this planet to die like The Colony."

"That's what happened there?"

She nodded. "There was an imbalance and everything died off. Maybe a couple thousand years ago, maybe a million. We don't really know. That's why we can't walk around outside of the bases without helmets for very long. The atmosphere sucks." She rapped her knuckles on the glass of hers. "But there used to be water on The Colony. Lots of it. They have fossils all over the place.

"And all the water just what? Disappeared?"

"Apparently."

"Wow. Okay. So, is it just hydrogen levels that are off here?"

"Hydrogen is low. Oxygen is high. The ocean's salinity level is fluctuating. It's like everything just went crazy. Weird, right?" I could see her frown, even through the helmet. "As if something is stealing hydrogen. The amount of water on the entire planet is down nearly two percent since we first received the disturbing data."

"Holy shit." That didn't sound like a lot, but when an entire planet's ecosystem was involved, that two percent would make a huge difference.

I took several of the sampling sticks and walked to the edge of the beach, looked out over the water. I wanted to go out there and swim. Feel the... wetness against my skin. The buoyancy. The shift and movement of the water. I couldn't deny it. But I wasn't a complete idiot. "Is it fresh or salt water?"

She thumbed toward the water. "Using Earth as a comparison, the water here is halfway between the two. Data shows freshwater streams, rivers and lakes that feed into this cove, and a vast body of salt water about the size of the Atlantic out there. So, in this cove, it's about half and half."

"Brackish, Got it." I smiled and tried to breathe it in, but the helmet didn't let me.

"So, no huge sharks out there?" I asked. Sharks, at least Earth sharks, lived in salt water. Alligators went for fresh water. But then there was Captain Hook and the giant

Seawater Crocodile that had taken his hand. Crocodiles loved brackish water on Earth. And they had no qualms about helping themselves to a tasty human. "Crocodiles? Giant squid? Any sort of space beasts out there that might eat us if we get too close to the edge?"

Rachel laughed. "Oh, yeah. No sharks. Squid, they'd be deep so I'm not really sure. As for here, I'll say probably not. The water is only about thirty or forty feet deep until you get out past the rocks. But animals aren't my turf. Giram!" she called.

A huge guy turned around, strode over. He was slightly taller than Surnen and Trax, and his shoulders were broader. Rachel introduced him to me as an Atlan. Holy shit, the guy was huge. "Any dangerous creatures out there in the water?"

His piercing dark eyes met mine. "None, my lady." While he was answering Rachel's question, he was looking at me. I realized then that both of us were to be called *my lady.* "I have been monitoring these coordinates for a week in preparation for our visit. No underwater data indicates any kind of life form that would be considered dangerous."

"Thank you," she replied. He bowed and returned to his task—which appeared to be watching over us while we worked—and I buried my disappointment at not being able to come face-to-face with a Valuri version of a dolphin or whale.

I helped Rachel with collecting samples, then watched as she analyzed them with some fancy space-age machinery. We worked over an hour and allowed the computer to process the data. As a team, we stared at the results.

"We were right. This planet is losing hydrogen. There is

more oxygen in the atmosphere than there was a week ago," she said, then looked around. "The question is, how? Why?"

"There's no data that indicates a specific location at issue," Giram replied. Two others in the group agreed.

"How can a planet just lose water? Is that even possible?" I asked, looking out over the murky color. "Unless..."

Everyone faced me, silently waiting for my possibility.

"I know you said you were monitoring the water level, but did you test the salinity or carbon dioxide levels in the water itself? What if it's not just hydrogen? What if, somehow, the ocean is actually losing water? Is the planet forming new, larger ice caps? Glaciers? Is the humidity higher? Something's wrong with the water cycle. I assume this planet has trackable weather patterns, and this close to water, the weather would be impacted by the water itself."

"You're saying that water is going where? Into a new North Pole?"

"I don't know yet, but would that account for the fluctuations in your readings?"

Rachel was quiet, then nodded. "It's an option to consider."

Everyone turned to face the ocean. "My expertise was in water contamination. Finding imbalances and cleaning up messes made by humans. But if this is some kind of natural planetary cycle, like an ice age or changing temperature in the planet's core, I'm not sure we can do anything to save the animals here."

"At least the planet is not inhabited. That would a much larger problem," Giram said.

I shrugged, not wanting to argue with a huge alien I barely knew. But to me, an extinction event on this planet—

on any planet—was a large problem. "Can I go and collect some samples from the water?"

Rachel nodded. "Absolutely. I'll run some data on ice formation and temperatures."

"I want to go under and look around."

"Under?" Giram asked, wide-eyed.

I nodded, tapped the glass of my helmet. "It's just like scuba."

The other scientists glanced at each other, clearly confused by the Earth abbreviation.

Rachel understood perfectly. "Great. I could do it but I'm a terrible swimmer and I don't like to get in water I can't see the bottom of." Rachel went to retrieve some sample vials and handed them to me.

She looked my space suit over from head to toe and grinned through her own helmet's visor. "Go ahead. Just don't take your suit off. We haven't done a full pathogen workup on this planet yet, and I don't want your skin peeling off or something."

Giram piped up. "As far as predators, there's nothing dangerous for at least half a mile from shore. Not here. That's why we chose this location for transport."

"Got it."

As the reddish water rolled up over the pink and white sand, it looked normal. Clear. Perfect. But the ocean that spread out before us was shades of red and orange. The depths that I could see in the distance looked a deep, dark purple. The water was unlike anything I had ever seen before, but it was stunning. Truly beautiful. The water was calm and smooth, the small waves barely cresting with tiny whitecaps as they moved onto shore.

Feeling lighter than I had in months, since the day I'd

realized what an idiot I'd been helping my so-called friends destroy those whaling ships, I carried two of the sampling sticks in one hand and waded hip-deep into the water. It wasn't the same as being in my wet suit dragging a longboard, but it felt glorious all the same. Just below the surface, giant white and yellow flowers floated like oversize lily pads the size of small cars. Tiny, sparkling fish darted under, over and around them, giving off tiny flashes of color that looked like twinkling diamonds had come to life. They swam around me, curious, swarming my legs so that I could no longer see my own feet as I stepped deeper into the calm water.

"You're sure I can go under in this thing?"

Rachel didn't even look up from what she was doing. "Yep. Full-on rebreather built into the suit and lights in the helmet. That suit is made to keep us alive in space, so the water is no big deal. We've got at least four more hours of air before we have to transport back."

"Sweet. And nothing that will eat me for at least half a mile."

"Well, unless Trax or Surnen shows up," Rachel called. "But I doubt you'd mind that all that much."

"You did not just say that out loud." I glanced over my shoulder as I stood waist-deep in the water to find Rachel completely unrepentant, a huge smile on her face.

"Did. And you know I'm right."

Refusing to answer, I appreciated the fact that the two Atlan warlords and four Prillon guards with us pretended not to hear our banter. They knew I was Surnen's mate. Knew I'd just arrived. I was big news. They were monitoring the perimeter, checking the sky, looking for danger and ignoring the fact that Rachel had just teased me

—within earshot—about having Surnen's or Trax's mouth on my—

"Mate. Are you well?" Surnen's voice echoed in my comms again, and I wanted to curse Rachel for the visual I couldn't get out of my head. "The readout on your suit shows abnormal external temperatures."

"I'm still fine, mate." Hungry for more hot sex, but other than that, completely normal. "I'm going to collect samples in the water."

"Is that safe?" he asked.

Giram spoke up, offering Surnen data he'd collected about the water. I was thankful he was trying to reassure him that I was fine.

"Very well," he replied, clearly appeased by the scientific data. "I am here if you need me."

Rachel cleared her throat. "Oh, she needs something, all right, but you can give it to her later, Doc. Along with that spanking you promised."

I could feel myself blush as I continued to walk deeper into the water. I turned around, faced the shore. "Good God. Could you at least pretend not to be listening, like the others?"

Rachel looked over her shoulder at the guards trying very hard to look anywhere but at the two of us. "Nope. I call it like I see it. And believe me, Maxim and Ryston don't like it when I go off world either." Her laughter chased me deeper into the water, and I turned back around and dived under, coming face-to-face with a large, shimmering eel-like creature with golden eyes and pink scales. The creature froze, terrified, before flashing away in a move I didn't even have a dream of following. Was I the first human they'd ever seen?

I drifted under the water, weightless once more, and I floated, truly free for the first time since I'd been arrested. I pressed a button on the vial and collected one sample, then tucked it into a pocket at my waist, then swam on. I had no flippers, so I kicked hard, my leg muscles working overtime. The burn felt good. Familiar. I was loving the helmet, the ability to breathe normally without anything in my mouth, without having to clear any water from goggles. Normally I had to stop at about eight feet, swallow hard and try to clear my ears of the pressure before I swam. But with the space suit, the pressure inside my suit remained constant. It was a scuba diver's dream.

Deeper and deeper I sank until the water's color was murky from the depth. I glanced up, guessing I was about thirty feet down. I wasn't sure if going any deeper would compress the air in my suit and use it up faster, as happened in scuba tanks on Earth. I doubted it, but I wouldn't risk using up all my air, so I didn't go any deeper. I didn't want to be sent home early like a misbehaving child on the playground.

I saw a fish that reminded me of a barracuda, long and thin, and followed it.

That was when I heard something unnatural, a rumble that had no place underwater. It was the hum of some kind of machine. Mechanical, like the sound of a pump on a fish tank. I knew what the water was supposed to sound like, the crash of waves, the sound of currents moving around rocks or coral, the quick, whiplike tail of an eel or a fish. I had even heard whales and dolphins speaking to one another back on Earth. Otherwise, below the surface the only thing I was supposed to hear was my breathing inside the suit. With a rebreather, there weren't even any bubbles floating back to the surface. I was a fish down here. Quiet as they were.

Nothing living was making that sound. I turned toward it, swam, then realized it was coming from the other direction, then whipped about. Paused.

"Rachel, can you hear that?" I asked, using my arms and legs to dive deeper into the water, swim a bit farther out. I didn't want to risk the oxygen, but I had to find out what was causing the noise.

Giram said I had half a mile until anything with big teeth would show up, and I was taking him at his word. I'd spent enough time in the water to know I was maybe a hundred meters from shore. The currents were stronger here, the water deeper, but not frightening. Nothing I couldn't handle. As long as the pressure this deep didn't affect my air supply.

"Hear what?"

"Listen. Can you hear that through my helmet?"

All chatter stopped between the guards and Rachel as they all listened. I held my breath so not even the sound of my breathing would interfere.

"It's a machine of some kind. Giram, you checked the water, right? You didn't discover this?"

"No, Lady Syrvon. Nothing shows on our equipment."

"Well, there's something down here. I can hear it." Or maybe I could feel it thrumming through my body like an echo? In the water, sound was different.

"Remain in position so we can scan." The Atlan ordered me to hold still, but that was pretty much impossible as I was floating in water at least three body lengths deep and the current was gently pulling me along the coastline away from Rachel and the team. It was nothing I couldn't handle, not like a riptide. The current was peaceful. Gentle. A short swim and I'd be back to them, or I could swim directly to the beach and walk back to their position.

"It's getting louder. Can you hear that?" I asked again.

"We hear it, Mikki," Rachel responded. "Come back to shore, and we'll adjust our scans for it. It should be easy to identify now."

I moved then, laying out flat and swimming for shore. I wasn't in a full-out sprint, but fast enough to get the hell out of the water. And I was out of shape. Seriously freaking out of shape. My lungs burned and so did my legs. I really should have done some more serious exercising the last few years.

"Why here?" I asked as I breathed hard. "Why this location? Extend your scans beyond this area."

"Already on it," Giram replied. "Scanning indicates a power source in the area of Lady Syrzon," Giram said. "By the gods, it's huge."

"That's not all, Warlord." Another voice came through the comms. "Similar pings throughout the water at even intervals. For hundreds of miles. There are thousands of them."

"Are you shitting me?" I asked, still trying to figure out what I had just kicked. My leg made contact with something, but when I looked, there was nothing but water and sand. Empty space. Whatever it was, the loud ping was like metal on metal and the reverberations traveled up my leg to my spine. Ouch.

"Mate, evacuate the water now." Surnen's voice in my ear was like a whip, startling me.

"Go. Go get her!" Rachel gave the order, and the ragged breathing of at least two of our guards came at me through the comms. I heard the panic in her voice. That was what had me giving up figuring out the object I'd hit and getting the hell out of the water.

"None of us can swim, my lady," Giram said.

"Are you fucking kidding me?" she snapped. "You survived the fucking Hive and you can't swim?"

I was still a good distance from shore, and I kicked hard. My foot struck metal again and another loud ping shot through my suit, loud enough this time to make my head swim for a moment. Risking a glance back I saw... nothing. Absolutely nothing.

What the hell? There had to be something there. Some kind of machine or something that made the noise. A submersible of some kind? Could it be invisible? Was that even possible?

I stopped for a moment, tried to catch my breath. Swinging around to get a closer look, I floated under the water and scanned the area with the light from my helmet. All I saw was water, and one small, swirling area of sand that looked like a little dirt devil on the bottom of the ocean floor. But the humming sound was much louder. "I can still hear it, but there's nothing to see. It makes no sense."

"What is it?" Rachel asked.

"I don't know. I think there's something on the bottom. I can take a closer look, but I'd rather not."

"Yes, female, do not," Giram said. "Return to shore. You've been successful in your search. The scanners can collect data now."

"Do you guys have technology to make something invisible?" I asked.

"Shit. Get out now, Mikki!" Rachel yelled and my heart leaped at the panic in her voice.

"Mate, evacuate the water," Surnen repeated. His voice was calm, but even at this great distance I felt his...terror through the collars.

Shit. What the hell had I found? Whatever it was, I wasn't going to get any closer. I wasn't an idiot. "Okay, I'm not lingering. I'm out of here."

"Hurry, Mikki. I don't like this." Rachel's concern goaded me to push through the burning in my lungs, but as hard as I tried to move, I wasn't gaining any ground.

"Something's wrong."

At that moment the humming noise grew in volume to a loud grind. Shit. The pull of the current became stronger and I kicked toward shore with every ounce of energy, but I wasn't getting anywhere. In fact, I was being pulled backward toward the sand.

I didn't panic underwater. Panic killed. But I was not happy about this. The invisible metal was creating suction behind me.

"Um, guys. It's pulling me down."

"What?" Rachel asked. "Kick. Swim. Do something!"

"Rachel, I'm fine. But I'm kicking as hard as I can, and I can't get away from it. It's pulling me to the bottom." I tried to keep my voice calm, but it was tough to do between panting for air and fighting off Surnen's panic. "Once I reach the bottom, I should be able to walk out of the current. I just have to ride it out."

"Fuck. Gods be damned. Get me the governor, now! We need transport!"

"Can you see anything?" Rachel asked.

One of the Prillon warriors was still yelling, but Rachel's voice was the only reasonable sound I could hear, so I focused on her.

"I can't *do* anything, Rachel. I'm letting it take me. It's strong. Like a rip. I have air. I'm fine." For now.

"A rip?"

"A rip current? Riptide?" Was she such a city slicker that she'd never heard of a rip current? Actually I had no idea where she was from. When I met her, just knowing she was from Earth had been more than enough.

"Oh God. You have to get out of there." She was losing her calm, but I couldn't afford to lose mine.

The odd current pulled me down fast, and my feet hit something hard several feet above the sandy bottom. It was like I was standing on solid water. I could feel the object, but I still couldn't see it. I lifted my foot, stomped down as best I could underwater. I knew the helmets had video recording of some kind, just like they had audio. "Can you see this? My foot? It looks like it's in the middle of open water, but I'm pushing against something solid. It feels like metal." I worked myself down to my hands and knees and knocked on it, rapping it with the knuckles of my space suit. The knocking sound pinging through something hollow was unmistakable. "See?"

"What's that swirling in the sand around the edges?" Rachel asked.

I glanced over the edge to the sandy ocean floor about a body length below me. "Some kind of whirlpool effect, I think. It's what's holding me down."

"Governor, she needs to get the fuck out of there now," Surnen snapped.

"This is Hive tech, my lady." Giram's voice was grim. "The energy signatures are newly registered, but it's Hive."

"Hive?" I repeated.

"Hive?" Surnen snarled.

"I have confirmed this is not the only unit of this kind in the water," Giram added. "You've only happened upon one of... ninety-four energy signatures in this cove alone."

"Ninety-four?" I repeated. Holy shit. Why here? Why on an uninhabited planet?

"There could be a transport mechanism on the inside." Rachel's voice was muffled for a moment; then I heard, "Captain, run a scan on water displacement under the surface. See if they are sucking up water."

"Why are you doing that?" Surnen asked Rachel. "Mikki, get to shore!"

It wasn't a whaling ship, but whatever this thing was, taking water off this planet wasn't good for the ecosystem here. I didn't know what kind of creatures lived here, but they had a right to live freely, to survive on their own damn planet. I knew that whatever was happening to the water, it was happening right under my feet.

It had pulled me right to it, like it truly was sucking the water through a great big straw. But where was it going? How did water transport, and in such quantities? Two percent of the planet's water had already been taken?

I had no intention of being stupid, but fighting a current was the easiest way to die and I had exactly zero chance of swimming up, away from this thing. Instead I felt my way to the edge of the platform, which appeared to be about ten feet wide, and used the downward pull of the water to sink to the ocean floor. I found what I was looking for on the bottom a few inches away, a rock twice the size of my fist. I picked it up and walked along the outer edge of the device, feeling my way with one gloved hand, until I felt a surge in water pressure pulling my arm toward the object.

Bracing myself against the hard side, I took position to

throw the rock toward the intake area. If this was where the water was going into the machine, the rock was definitely big enough to throw a huge wrench in the works. At least, that's what I was hoping. If I could block the suction somehow, I could swim away from this thing without having a heart attack. I really, *really* needed to start exercising more.

"Here goes nothing." I said.

"What the fuck are you doing?" Surnen asked.

"Mikki? This is Maxim. You will return to shore and join the others for transport back to The Colony immediately."

"I'm trying," I replied. This thing—or ninety-four of them—was more than I could solve on my own.

With adrenaline pumping through me, I tried to throw the rock toward the strong pull of water.

A loud *clang* had me making a fist in victory as I pushed myself back, then a little farther, away from the main pull of the machine. The flow of water holding me here weakened, and I didn't waste any time moving away. I sensed at once when I was out of its reach and began to swim toward shore. "It worked. On my way."

The sound changed all of a sudden, a loud *boom* making me wince inside my helmet.

"Fuck," Giram snapped. "There was an energy spike. Something is happening out there."

No kidding. A whirring noise replaced what had been a quiet hum, and the suction returned several times as strong. So fucking strong I couldn't gain any ground despite the fact that I was halfway to the surface. It was pulling me back. I used my arms, kicked, but I was caught in the suction. "It's working harder now. It's caught me, and I'm being pulled toward it. It's sucking me in!"

"Find her exact coordinates and transport her out. Now!" Maxim snapped.

"There's no transport beacon. The suit is not military grade."

I could hear voices arguing in my comms, but I was breathing hard, trying to fight the machine's power. If it was sucking water from the planet and transporting it somewhere, I didn't want to go wherever the water was going. Especially if it was being taken by the Hive.

Shit. This was going to be bad.

urnen, The Colony

I STORMED out of the medical unit, tossing a tray of supplies to the side in my haste. I'd been listening in on the mission to Valuri but focusing on Mikki. I didn't really give a shit what Giram was doing unless it impacted my mate. Now I knew what an Atlan who let his beast take over felt like. Out of control. Wild. Feral. Insane.

No one should get in my way or I'd rip his head off. My mate was in danger, and I had to get to her. Now.

I'd been hesitant to let Mikki go to Valuri. On a male level I was a selfish bastard. She'd only been mine overnight. I'd had my hands on her for such a short time, my fingers itched to touch her again. My cock was hard with the need to bury deep inside her. My balls were full and aching to empty every drop of cum into her pussy. Mark her.

Remind her and everyone else she came upon that she belonged to me. I needed her. Craved her like a drug.

A day ago I hadn't even known of her existence, but now, *my* existence revolved around her. The collars would permit nothing less. I wasn't in love with her, not yet. But she was *mine*, and I was fiercely possessive. Protective, and yet I'd let her go. Ever since my parents died, I'd closed myself off. My heart. My mind. I'd vowed to never again let another in. I'd followed protocol and put my ass in the testing chair, but hadn't expected anything, or anyone, to come of it. It had been required. The hope of a match? Slim.

So slim I'd pretty much forgotten the possibility. Until yesterday. Until I'd let myself become weak and vulnerable. But now... hearing that Mikki was in trouble, *feeling* her every emotion from the fucking bottom of an ocean on another planet? I was wild. What I'd felt for my parents and then their loss was nothing compared to this... this ferocity I had for Mikki.

"Get the fuck out of my way!" I yelled, racing down the corridor. The stripe on the wall changed from green to blue to red, indicating I was making headway across the base to the transport room, yet it felt like I would never get there. Mikki was down there, underwater with a Hive mechanism of some kind. Stuck. Caught.

She was captured by the Hive, in a trap of sorts, even unintentionally. If they got their integrated hands on her...

I listened to the voices of the crew on Valuri through the comms unit embedded next to my NPU. "Someone needs to get out there and help her," Rachel practically shouted. "Do we have rope?"

"Giram, call on your beast and just pull her away," I said.

He was Atlan. He could just go out there and get her. Surely the water would part for him or something.

"Doctor, I can't swim and neither can my beast," Giram admitted. It seemed we had found his weakness.

Gods, mine too. I couldn't swim either. There was water on Prillon Prime, but it wasn't used for amusement like on Earth. Water was drunk. Bathed in. Looked at. Prillon Prime's oceans harbored very dangerous creatures, and I'd never even considered the idea of getting in it.

"I can swim," Rachel said. "I'll go get her."

"I forbid it," Maxim snapped. "You are not strong enough to pull her from whatever that machine is. If Mikki can't get herself free, all you'll do, mate, is get yourself caught as well."

"Where the fuck are you, Surnen?" Trax shouted. "Fuck, get to transport or I'm leaving without your ass."

I came upon a sharp turn in the corridor, all but rammed into the wall, then pushed off and pivoted to continue on. "Thirty seconds," I breathed. "Get the transport ready so it will start as soon as I step onto the pad."

"Always late. I'll go now. You catch up."

"NO!" I bellowed. Warriors even bigger than me stopped in their tracks and pressed themselves against the wall to let me pass. "I must get to her. How could this happen? Protocols were in place."

"We weren't expecting the Hive, Doctor. Not on an uninhabited planet like this one," Giram replied.

"I don't give a fuck," I practically growled. "The Hive should always be taken into account. Every scenario, every incident. They should never be taken for granted."

"I'm caught, but I'm fine, Surnen," Mikki said. "I'm just hanging out here, waiting."

Her voice had that sharp bite I was accustomed to, but she wasn't bickering with me. She was fighting an unknown machine that held her trapped beneath the water. I sensed calmness in her, but fear as well. She had oxygen; her sensors hadn't indicated otherwise. There was only so much. Her supply of air would run out eventually. And this was her first contact with the Hive, even if only tangentially. This was perhaps worse, for we knew nothing about what they were doing with the planet. Why they were using the water. Where it was going. Where she'd go if she was pulled into the transporter beneath the sea.

"You're not *fine*," I snapped. "You should be here on The Colony in my bed. Tied to it so I know you're safe."

"Tied to it?" she snapped. "Is this part of your protocols? Is it tradition to be tied to a bed like that? Because I might need to find a new planet."

"It should be," Maxim said, his voice coming through clear but grim and determined. "If you go near that water, mate, that is where you will find yourself as well."

"Hey!" Rachel replied.

"If it were protocol, you'd be safe right now instead of using up all the reserve oxygen in your suit," I told Mikki. "You're below fucking water on a strange planet that has never been visited. There is no protocol for that."

"I have three hours of oxygen remaining," Mikki replied. "I have my feet braced. I'm not going into the machine, whatever it is. There's no fucking way I'm being transported by the Hive."

Those words only ratcheted up my panic threefold. I knew what it was like to be transported by the Hive. So did every other fighter listening in. "We will get you out of there, and then you are never leaving our quarters again. Never!"

"Surnen," Mikki said. "I'm fine. We'll figure this out. If you'd stop shouting, we could—"

"Do not diminish this," I yelled back. "I won't let anything happen to you. I can't. I won't survive. Rules are instituted for a reason. Strict regulations and protocols ensure issues are analyzed and risk assessed. They were supposed to keep you safe, but they haven't."

"I'm not at risk, Surnen," she countered. "And don't you dare say the match was based on protocol and regulations."

The transport room door slid open, and I jumped all the steps to the raised platform to stand beside Maxim, Trax and three more warriors carrying equipment. The hum and vibration of imminent transport was loud in the room, heavy beneath my boots.

"Now!" I shouted, looking to the tech. Why hadn't we left yet?

"Helmet," he replied, and Trax handed me mine. The others already had theirs locked into place. I twisted mine into place and nodded the moment the lock clicked.

From one blink to the next, we were on Valuri. My body ached, the twist of transport stabbing in my skull, but I only blinked and ignored it, took in the initial crew around me. I spun about, my feet now in soft sand, and looked out at the ocean. It looked peaceful. Calm. Tranquil. It was a different color than the images I'd seen of Mikki's water on Earth, but the reddish hue was appealing, nonetheless.

Yet beneath the surface...

"Where is she?"

Everyone pointed in the same direction, just to the right of where we stood.

I started toward her, running made difficult in the soft sand, but Trax grabbed my arm, stopped me with a strong yank. "You can't just rush into the water."

"Watch me," I snarled, trying to shrug off his hold.

"Surnen," he said, gripping my shoulder. "An actionable plan is being put in place."

I shook my head. "Actionable? No. We don't wait. We go now. I won't let this happen again. This can't happen again." Shrugging off his hold, I moved toward the water only to be stopped by Trax's arm around my waist.

"Stop."

"I can't. I can't lose her. I can't go through this again." I shoved him away and ran.

He followed me, frowned. "What are you talking about? *Again*?"

"My mother," I breathed. "I won't let Mikki die, too." I couldn't breathe. The suit was too hot. Too close. Too tight. Fuck!

I ripped the helmet off my head and threw it to the sand. "Mikki!" The water was around my ankles when Trax tackled me.

"Put your gods-damned helmet back on."

"I can't breathe." I rolled him off me and waded deeper into the water, shouting for my mate. She was out there. Dying.

"Giram!" Maxim yelled something at the Atlan, but they were behind me. Mikki, my Mikki, was in front of me. Dying. Leaving me alone.

"Surnen, stop. That's an order." Maxim yelled the command, but I was deaf to anything but the pounding in my chest, in my head. She was going to die because I hadn't stopped her. Because I let her go on this mission. Because I didn't follow protocol.

Mikki wasn't approved for this kind of work. She should never have been transported here. Never.

I'd failed her. Just like my fathers had failed my mother.

"Mikki!"

My ribs felt like they were collapsing, squeezing me until my heart could no longer beat, my lungs unable to fill with air. My vision blurred with tears as I fought to hold on to hope, knowing I was going to lose her just like I'd lost everyone else.

I'd be alone again. I didn't want to live without her. I couldn't go back.

I walked deeper into the water, the waves lapped against to my chest. "Mikki!"

"You're a fucking idiot, you know that?" Trax appeared as if out of nowhere, and this time he wasn't alone. Giram had gone beast, the huge bastard's arms wrapped around me, clamping my arms to my sides.

I kicked. Thrashed. I threw my head back and crashed my skull against Giram's helmet. Hot, wet blood trickled down the back of my skull. I struck again. I had to get to Mikki.

"Surnen! Calm the fuck down." Trax grabbed my face by the chin and squeezed, hard, forcing me to look at him. "Don't make me shoot your ass."

"Let me go."

"No. You are losing your fucking mind. Giram is going to carry you back to shore, and you are going to fucking stay there while I go get our mate." Trax slammed my helmet back on my head, initiated a pathogen scan and nodded at Giram. "Thanks. Take him back."

Giram turned and I saw the other guards with Rachel and Maxim, the female gaping at me like I'd lost my damn mind. I had lost more than that. I had nothing without Mikki.

"Surnen? I'm fine. Okay? I'm not going anywhere. We have time to figure this out." Mikki's voice was pure sweetness and light, and I broke, slumping in Giram's hold moments before he dumped me on the sand like a bag of rocks.

I deserved worse.

Trax bent down, taking a knee to look me in the eyes. "Now, tell me what the hell that was about."

"My mother."

"You've never talked about her or your fathers. Not once in all the years I've known you."

"The past should stay in the past."

"Perhaps, but not today."

"I'm so sorry. What happened to your mother?" Mikki said, her voice coming through loud and clear over all our comms.

"My mother was rebellious," I clarified. "Free-spirited. They were all sickened by a deadly disease they never should have been exposed to—all because my mother had wanted to take home a harmless-looking flower from a newly discovered world. My fathers allowed her to break the rules and hide the plant in her gear. She smuggled it back to our home on Prillon Prime. Turns out, it harbored a deadly virus carried by alien insects hidden in the stems. She was dead within a week. My fathers followed her two days later."

I heard her gasp.

"All because they broke the rules."

"And so you decided never to break them," Trax sighed. "Well, that explains a lot."

"*Protocol saves lives.* Rules are rules for a reason."

"I'm not down here because your dads didn't follow the rules, Surnen," Mikki said, her voice calm. "Things happen. Sometimes things completely out of our control. Uh-oh."

All around me, chimes erupted from every scanner and handheld device.

"Sensors picking up additional energy coming from the machines," one of the warriors called. His gaze was on the scanner in his hand.

Rachel waved a scanner at her mate. "The machines are what's bringing this about. It's not a climate issue. The planet will be bled dry of all water in months at this rate. Maxim, we have to do something."

Trax looked to me, his rust-colored gaze narrowed. "They're sucking the life from this planet."

"Mikki, do you see? You shouldn't have gone down there," I snapped. "There's no protocol for going under the fucking water!"

"I.C. Core Command, this is Governor Maxim of The Colony. Get me Helion. Now!" he snapped.

"Request denied. Location could not be verified. You are not on The Colony," a benign voice replied.

"I am on Valuri," Maxim said, going over to Rachel and standing directly beside her, close enough that they touched from shoulder to thigh. I doubted he would leave her side before we were off this planet. "Your data will confirm that. It will also confirm a Hive presence that had been undetected by your commander. Get me Helion now or I will have you working as a prison guard orbiting Everis before the sun sets."

"Um, guys..." Mikki said. "The suction is picking up. It's like it switched into high gear."

Her voice was muffled by the swirl of water, the loud vibration of a machine we hadn't even known existed until minutes ago.

"We need to get her out of there," Trax said. "Now!"

"No one can swim but Rachel, and she's not going out there," Maxim said, stating the obvious.

"We can use a transport beacon," I said, considering the simplest solution.

The governor nodded and came over to me, slapped one in my palm.

On The Colony, there were rules and protocols in place for everything. Within the Coalition, warriors survived by rules.

Mikki's voice came through, even a little muffled. "You guys fight wars in space, but no one learns how to swim? That doesn't sound very smart to me. Don't any of the other planets have water on them?"

I could breathe again, and Mikki's scolding actually made me grin. "Prillon Prime has large oceans, mate. But the water is ruled by many deadly predators. We do not swim because we do not go into the water."

"Don't you have lakes? Swimming pools?"

I looked at Trax, who shrugged. "I'm going in."

We stared at the water, whose surface was completely calm even though we could hear the machinery through Mikki's comms. The beeping through the data scanners confirmed it was anything but placid beneath the surface. I felt helpless. Just as useless as I had when my family had died and I could do nothing to save them.

"I'll go," I said, determined. I'd die a slow death if Mikki didn't make it.

Trax looked around. "No. You're out of your head. I'll go."

"How?" I practically shouted, raising my arms in the air.

While I was fighting down another bout of rising panic, Trax was becoming sharp and focused. This was a situation he recognized, and it had nothing to do with water. There was a problem that needed solving with action. The Hive was the enemy, and he knew battle better than most.

Trax's gaze narrowed as he faced away from the beach, away from our mate who was slowly—or possibly very quickly—being sucked into some kind of water transport system directly to the Hive.

"Give me the transport beacon." Mindlessly I held my hand out, and he took it from me and stuck it in a pocket. "I'll surf."

What? With those words, he sprinted toward the nearest trees, disappearing into the thick foliage, only to return seconds later with a huge piece of wood. It was about a foot shorter than he was, but sturdy and thick. If he weren't a Prillon, he might not be able to carry it. It was stripped of bark and branches, rotting in places. A dead tree, slowly rotting back into the ground.

"Are you crazy?" I called as he ran toward the water. "You're not accustomed to being on land, let alone in water. It's going to sink and take you with it!"

He didn't slow down or turn. His feet hit the water, and he tossed the log out in front of him, creating a splash and a huge ripple. It dipped beneath the surface, then bobbed. He looked over his shoulder and shouted, "You're right. I can't relate to being on a planet, on real ground. I sure as fuck know nothing about an ocean. I do know about being a mate. She needs our help, and I'm going to give it. No matter what. I might not be able to swim, but I can save our mate. *I can.*"

He grabbed the end of the log and pulled it back so he was standing beside it, the water level with his waist. He leaned forward so his chest was centered on it, legs and arms on either side, just as we'd seen in the comm videos of Rachel and the surfing competitions from Earth. There were no waves, thank fuck, but Trax had no idea what he was doing. He moved his arms and legs like we'd seen on the vids, and he somehow propelled himself farther out into the water without falling off or sinking.

While he had his helmet on and a full supply of oxygen, if he went under and didn't find Mikki, there would be no other way to save her. If he couldn't get the transport beacon to her, she was as good as dead.

rax

I HAD no fucking idea what I was doing. I was floating on a log, frantically kicking my legs and moving my arms in something similar to what I'd seen Mikki do in those comm vids. She'd propelled herself across the surface gracefully, as if one with the ocean.

I didn't feel as in sync, but I wasn't sinking. I was surprisingly buoyant, as if there was no gravity. The log undulated with the movement of the water's surface, and if I wasn't concerned about a rescue or that I might drown, it was rather peaceful. A small roll in the surf came and dipped the front of the log, and I took a bunch of water right in my face.

I shut my eyes, afraid, but realized I was protected.

Thank fuck we had to arrive wearing our helmets. Mikki was some thirty feet down, and I had to get off this bobbing tree trunk and get to her. I'd be dead in seconds without the protection—and oxygen—the helmet provided. There was no way the makers of the piece of the Coalition-required uniform thought it would be put to this kind of use. We fought the Hive in space, not beneath the ocean.

"Mate, how are you faring?" I asked, water splashing onto the glass, leaving droplets in my vision.

"It's like a huge fan or vacuum cleaner. There's no way I can get away from it. I've got my feet braced on either side, the main opening is only about three feet wide. It's sucking in sand and water, plant life. Everything. I'm going to... I can reach a rock. I'll try and see if I can break it."

"Don't move," I shouted over the sound of the water.

"I got one." A metallic clang followed by an awful sound came through the comms that made me wince.

"Mate!" Surnen shouted.

"I'm fine, but that didn't do anything. And I almost lost my hand."

"Cease at once."

"Already ceased, mate. Trust me. I don't want to be eaten alive by an underwater Shop-Vac."

"What the fuck is a Shop-Vac?"

"I'll explain later." Mikki's laughter kept me moving. She wasn't hurt. I was getting closer. All I needed was time.

"No change to status, Governor." Giram's voice came through loud and clear as I continued to smack at the water and work my way farther from shore. Closer to Mikki.

I sensed her concern now. She was stuck. Not pinned, but a strong pull was holding her on the bottom of the water. A pull that could be tied to a larger machine that fed the vast network that was sucking water from the planet.

"I'm coming, mate," I said.

"Um... Trax... no. You can't."

"Drop there, Trax," Rachel said. "You're directly above her."

I glanced back at shore as another wave rolled over me. My suit was impervious to water, but other than floating in space, I'd never felt so small. Insignificant. A tiny speck of nothing at the mercy of the gods. I gripped the log tightly, knowing it was the only thing keeping me on the surface now. I had to let go. I had to get to Mikki.

I just had to hope that my lack of swimming abilities would actually help me sink right to her.

"Look up, mate," I said. "I'm dropping to you in three... two... one."

I rolled off the log, and I sank below the surface instantly. I was heavy and far from buoyant. For the first time in years, I prayed to the gods as the water engulfed me. The world was now a rust color. Fish swam by, skittering away at my actions.

"The water is pulling me down." It was just as I'd expected. The vacuum created by the machine was taking me right to her.

"I see you getting closer. You're almost to me."

"I see you," I said when she appeared through the reddish haze of the water.

Relief swamped the collars. Mine, Mikki's. Even Surnen's.

"I'm straddling the vacuum. If you can, be sure to brace your feet, but not between mine."

"Got it," I said, back in control. Mikki was here. She was an underwater expert, but it was my job to get the Hive machine to stop long enough for us to get away.

When I stood before her, I looked down at her face.

Fuck, so familiar. So mine. I wanted to grab her in for a hug and never let go. Underwater wasn't the time or place.

"I'm getting you the fuck out of here, and then I'm going to kiss you," I told her.

She grinned, her wide smile visible through the glass. "And I'm going to let you."

"Um, guys, kiss later. Survive now," Rachel said.

"Surviving would be great," Surnen said. "Governor, where is I.C.? If I can't help get Mikki out of there, then I can at least coordinate from land."

"Helion's on his way, whatever that means," the governor practically growled. It didn't seem like our leader liked the guy.

I looked to Mikki, who was also listening. She had no idea who Helion was. I didn't either, but I did know I.C.

"I'm glad they're coming, but once they get here, they're going to want as much information as we can give them," Surnen stated. "Rachel, get as many samples as you can. The Fleet will need to know if these Hive machines are having any other effects on the planet. Giram, work with the others. Grid the Hive energy signatures that we are aware of. I doubt they've taken enough water to destabilize the planet's orbit, but get a team on that as well." I felt Surnen's control snap back in place. "Trax, get our mate the fuck out of there."

I winked at Mikki, and she rolled her eyes. The pull from the Hive machine was strong. I could feel it working my leg muscles and expected Mikki to be growing weary. I remembered feeling those sinewy muscles. She was strong. But for how long?

Reaching into my pocket, I pulled out the transport beacon, slapped it onto Mikki's shoulder, although the movement was as if I were pushing through thick breakfast porridge, the water making my hand move slower than normal.

While it affixed itself to Mikki's suit, the light didn't come on. I pushed the button. Nothing. "Fuck. I think it's broken."

"Are you fucking kidding me?" Surnen shouted. I knew he was giving a death glare to the governor.

"The energy signature of the Hive device is interfering with transport. The techs cannot get a lock on the beacon's location." Maxim's explanation did not make me happy, but I had Mikki in my arms and we were both alive and breathing. I wasn't going to give up yet.

"Okay, mate. Any suggestions?" I asked Mikki, keeping my voice calm. I tried to slow my breathing. We weren't exactly safe, but we could pause for a moment. Think.

She pointed to the sandy sea bottom. I couldn't miss the pull of everything into the ground. I couldn't see the machinery that was at work.

Picking up my foot, I stomped down, heard the sound of metal, felt it.

"The rock worked," she said. "It messed with the gears or whatever it is. If there was something bigger to shove in there, it might stop the suction long enough for us to get away."

We looked around us. No more rocks, nothing but small plants that leaned inward toward the suction, their roots too sturdy to be pulled in.

"My helmet," I said. "I can take it off, jam it in there."

"What? That's crazy. You need *air*."

"Not if it stops and we can swim to the surface."

"The idea has merit," Surnen said. "The helmet has a

shield rating of nine point seven and can withstand direct fire from an ion cannon."

"You're saying jamming it into a Hive machine will not crush it," I replied.

"Hopefully not. If their intention was to displace water, I doubt the machinery is built that strong."

"But you won't have air," Mikki said. "We can use mine. I can hold my breath longer. I'm used to being caught underwater."

I shook my head. "Mate. No. It must be my helmet."

"What? Why?"

"Because I will not risk your life," I said. I was calm now. My mission resolute. This was what I was meant to do, why I had gone through training, been captured by the Hive, integrated. Sent to The Colony. Became Surnen's second.

My fate, my destiny had always been to be here and to save Mikki.

"You'll risk yours?"

"That is why Prillons mate in pairs. If something happens to one, you still have a mate to protect you. Surnen will choose another second. You will be taken care of, I promise you."

"You're fucking insane. No. That is not okay."

"Mate. *Mate*."

I could feel Mikki's panic, so I grabbed her shoulders. "Feel the pull of the machine. It's not stopping."

"We'll wait it out. It seems to stop and start."

"For how long? Until we both run out of air? We have no alternative. The transport beacon didn't work. The energy signature of this machine is blocking the signal. There is no other way out of here."

"But I'm used to being underwater. You're not."

"And that is why I trust you. I might save you, but you will need to save me right back. I have never been in water before, and I don't know how to swim."

I grinned at her. It took a moment, but she grinned back. "Funny, not funny?"

"Nothing about this is amusing, I assure you."

Taking a deep breath, she sighed. "Okay. Here's how this will work. We're thirty feet down. Once you take off that helmet, you're going to have to remain calm and do exactly what I'm about to tell you. Ever held your breath underwater before?"

"No."

"Well, welcome to Scuba 101."

"I was worried we had nothing in common," I admitted, needing her to know in case something went wrong. "That I couldn't understand the world you came from."

"You can now?"

"Yes. It is peaceful beneath the water. Quiet. Beautiful. I understand why you would love this." I looked around at the murky depths of the ocean. "But let us find something in common on land, all right?"

Peace swamped me. Acceptance. I'd never felt anything this powerful before, and it was all coming from her. My mate. "I offer myself as your second. I vow to protect you with my life, to kill for you, to die for you, to do all in my power to see to your happiness."

"Now is not the time, Trax." Surnen's stern reprimand echoed in my helmet—and Mikki's—but I didn't care. She needed to know. I was hers, without regrets, for as long as I lived.

Warmth swamped me through the collar. Perhaps not love, not yet, but something so close I could not determine what the difference might be. Surnen must have felt it too, for Mikki's emotions silenced him. "I accept. You are both insane, do you know that?"

"We are yours, Mikki. Perhaps now you fully understand what that means." I spoke slowly, clearly, as I knew Surnen would understand the need that drove me.

"Perhaps. Now let's get out of here." Mikki closed off her emotions until there was no warmth, no fear, only calm the likes of which I'd only ever sensed from other warriors on the battlefield. Or Surnen in surgery.

I nodded. This was a side of our female I had never seen before, and it fascinated me.

"Once the helmet's off, you won't be able to see. The pressure of the water is going to make it feel like your ears are about to explode. It's going to hurt. Hold your nose and blow air into your sinus cavities; try to equalize the pressure inside your head with the water pressure pushing down on you."

"So, like losing my helmet in space, but in reverse."

She blinked, thinking. "I guess that makes sense. So, yes. You must remain calm. Step one, take a deep breath, fill your lungs with air. Step two, remove the helmet and equalize the pressure in your ears so your eardrums don't rupture. Do you even have eardrums?"

"Yes, mate. Our ears are very similar to human ears in both structure and function." Surnen's words made her sigh in relief.

"Good. Okay. Step three, since you won't be able to see anything, I'll take the helmet from you and try to jam it into the machine. If it works, I'll grab your hand, and we'll kick for the surface."

"I understand." I didn't like the sound of it, but I'd

survived worse in space, and far worse at the hands of the Hive. I could endure far more pain than damaged ears if it meant saving our mate. "I am ready."

"No. Wait. What if it doesn't work? You'll drown."

"Mate, it will work." I had expected to die in some Hive battle. I'd expected to die a Hive prisoner. I never imagined, ever, to die at the bottom of an ocean. Dying here was not my destiny. I had to be positive. There was no alternative.

"Okay, it will work. It has to work. You'll have to bend your knees and push off the ground. Pretend you're trying to jump up in the air, that should help propel you to the surface. If it doesn't work, fight the pull. Keep your legs mostly straight and kick. Kick hard and fast. Put your arms over your head and pull down, like this."

Mikki demonstrated and I recognized the moves. "Like I did with my log."

"Exactly."

"All right, let's do it." I lifted my hands toward my helmet.

"Wait."

I stilled.

"We're thirty feet down. The air is pressurized. You have to slowly exhale as you rise. Blow out slowly, releasing the air as it expands. If you don't, your lungs will explode."

This just kept getting better. "Explode?"

"Maybe not explode completely, but it'll be bad."

"So you have protocols in place. Rules that must be followed in order to survive?"

I could see she mentally paused, watched as her mind worked. "Absolutely. Diving is dangerous. You have to follow the rules. If you don't, you die."

I arched a brow and just stared at her. Waited.

I felt the moment she understood. Surnen's need for rules, his obsession with them. From what he'd admitted, his parents had broken them and they'd died. Mikki had fought them her whole life, but she'd been following them in her passion and hadn't even realized.

"Oh," she practically whispered.

"You understand now?" I asked softly.

She nodded. "I do. Surnen, I'm sorry for fighting you so hard." Shame, sadness, compassion filled me through the collar. Regret. Acceptance. And that warm feeling again, this time for Surnen as well as myself, and much stronger than before.

"Mate, now is *not* the time for this," Surnen said, his command loud and clear even this far under the water. He was being strong, holding himself together. Controlling his emotions, just as Mikki was doing. I was the weak link here, drowning in pride for our female.

"Trax, do as she orders. Follow the protocols needed to survive and get the hell out of there."

Mikki and I stared at each other. Resolute. This was it.

"Just don't panic when your ears feel like they're going to explode. Kick off the ground and slowly breathe out," she said. "Okay?"

"Mate," I said. "I am proud that you are mine."

"Trax, you're... well, mine. And don't forget it for one second."

"Never." With that, I set my hands on my helmet and turned it, unlocking the seal.

Instantly water rushed in. My breath was caught in my body. My face was wet. Pressed upon. It was cold, but not as cold as deep space. I opened my eyes for a second, only saw a red blur. I felt as if daggers stabbed at my ears, but I held on to the helmet, afraid to drop it and ruin our plan.

I couldn't hear anything beyond the pain.

The helmet was ripped from my fingers.

I did as Mikki had instructed and held my nose, blew air into my sinus cavity until the pain lessened, became manageable.

All at once I could feel the suction of water release, hear the grind of gears. We were free. It had instantly worked, the Hive machine stalling enough for us to break free of its hold. I didn't wait. I bent my knees and did exactly as Mikki had instructed and pushed off the sea floor. I lifted up and kept going. Higher and higher, using my arms, kicking my legs. Mikki gripped my forearm and tugged as I slowly let out air.

My chest burned as I ran out of air to exhale. My eyes were squeezed shut as I thrashed and fought for the surface, but I had no idea how far there was to go. How I could survive a second longer holding my breath.

All at once, we broke the surface, and I gasped, bobbed on top of the water, then started to sink again. Mikki's hold tugged me back to the surface. I blinked water out of my eyes, saw her talking but couldn't hear a word since I had no helmet. Looking to shore, I saw everyone waving their arms. Mikki was tugging on me, shifting to her back and kicking. I mimicked her, rolling onto my back as well. It was easier this way. I floated, somehow. Water splashed over my face, but I was used to it... a little, now.

I felt arms beneath my shoulders, and I dropped, my feet hitting ground. Mikki stood up, and we were surrounded, fifteen feet from shore, by the others.

Mikki undid her helmet, dropped it into the water. She

grinned at me. I felt her happiness, her relief through the collars. "Fuck, mate," I said. "Let's never do that again."

She laughed and launched herself at me. Kissing me. Hugging me. I was never letting go.

Surnen was beside us, touching Mikki's shoulder, her wet hair. Our kiss ended, and he pulled her into his arms, kissing her, holding her. His relief amplified my own until I was nearly giddy with the bizarre bubbling happiness flowing through my entire body.

"Governor, control your people. You now have three who have been exposed to potentially dangerous pathogens. Your group will transport off this planet in thirty seconds. Quarantine them until an assessment has been completed."

That arrogant, asshole voice had to be Helion's. No one else would dare speak to Maxim in that tone.

I lifted my head, looked to shore. There was a group of seven or eight Prillon warriors, all wearing identical black uniforms and stern expressions beneath their helmets. They must be the I.C. and must have just transported to the beach.

"Helion, glad you're here," Maxim replied. "It seems like you've got a Hive problem on Vulari."

He walked out of the water holding Rachel's hand. I pulled Mikki along, and everyone moved to shore, Surnen right beside us. He had yet to say anything, but his emotions were turbulent, barely controlled. Silence was probably wise, since I wasn't sure Surnen would be able to control his mouth if Helion dared say a word about our female.

"I'll get my crew out of here, especially since three of them have removed their helmets. Keep me updated on these Hive machines. I have a member of The Colony who's an expert on underwater skills, if you have need."

"No," Surnen and I said at the same time. Then we were gone, transported away, the sound of the governor's laugh and the I.C. commander's gruff shout the last we heard.

I didn't give a shit about I.C. or their problems. I had my mate. She was safe. She was ours. And I wasn't letting her go again. I wasn't letting anything get in my way of loving her. Even my own stupid insecurities. I'd left them all at the bottom of the ocean.

12

*S*urnen, *The Colony, Private Quarters*

THE BED MAY HAVE BEEN SIZED for three, but the shower tube in my quarters was not. It didn't even fit two, which meant we stood outside the enclosure and watched as Mikki washed the Valurian ocean from her body.

We'd been escorted directly to my quarters and instructed to remain under quarantine until one of my medical staff cleared us. Which was just fine with me. I had no intention of leaving Mikki's side anytime soon.

We'd stripped her bare and pushed her into the tiny tube, then removed our own sodden clothes.

We hadn't been back on The Colony for ten minutes. It had all happened so fast. No, not just the fucking mess on Valuri, but everything.

"It hasn't even been a day," I murmured. We should have felt silly standing side by side and doing nothing but staring at our mate as she washed her hair, but I didn't. Neither of us could look away, as if she'd disappear.

As if she'd never actually been here in the first place.

But she had. I was different. Holy fuck, I'd been ripped from my bland, strict existence and thrust into hell.

We all had, and we'd survived.

Mikki's mind was calm. Quiet. The rush of adrenaline had faded from her system. It had from Trax's as well, but he was restless, body and mind. I had to wonder if it was because she was used to danger, found a thrill in it, while Trax did not. He'd been in dangerous situations throughout his career as a warrior, was used to battle, to risking his life, but not what he'd just endured.

I'd only been in the water for less than a minute, and I hadn't gone beneath the surface. The idea of it, the reminder that my mate had been trapped down there, had me panicking even now, far from Valuri and its body of water. Whatever the fuck was in that ocean was Helion's problem.

Mine was before us, and she wasn't a problem at all.

"Amazing, isn't it?" he said. "I had no idea."

The water turned off, the drying setting began, and within seconds the door slid open and Mikki stepped out onto the mat. Grabbing a bath sheet from a hook, I wrapped it about her, then pulled her into my arms. She was so small, her head only coming up to my chest. She offered no resistance, instead wrapping her arms about my waist and hugging me right back. Her covering fell to the floor.

Trax climbed into the tube and took his turn as we stood there. I was hard, no doubt she could feel the insistent prod against her torso, but I did nothing about it. My cock could wait.

"Mate," I breathed, leaning down and kissing the top of her damp head.

"Scan me for injuries."

I stiffened and felt a rush of panic. Setting my hands on her shoulders, I pushed her back, tipped my chin down to look at her. "You're hurt?"

"No, I feel fine, but I know you want to check with your little wands." She circled her finger in the air. "I'll submit to a medical test. Whatever you need to be reassured."

Trax stepped out of the tube, and I looked to him. He'd heard what she said, and I saw the heat in his gaze, but also... affection. Respect. Adoration.

I felt all of it, too. Her concern. Her need for me to be happy.

"Come here, mate. Let Surnen rinse the sea from his skin."

It was my turn, but I didn't want to leave her, even by stepping into the bathing tube for the short time it took to wash. By the time I was done, Trax had led her from the room, and he was sitting on the side of the bed, she upon his lap.

Fuck. She was so beautiful, so perfect.

Such a tiny thing and she was fierce. Brave.

Mikki looked up at me when I entered. "I want you to test me."

I studied her, felt her emotions through the collars.

"All right." I grabbed a wand from my medical kit by the entry door and returned. "Lay on the bed."

Trax stood, keeping her in his arms, pivoted and gently set her down in the center. Crawling up beside her, he settled himself along her length, propped up on one elbow.

Using the simple scanner, I waved it over her body from

head to toe. While I watched the readings that came
through, I also looked over every inch of my mate. I saw the
scars she'd mentioned, the tan lines. Her nipples pebbled,
and she licked her lips.

"Mate," I said, feeling her arousal grow. It made my cock
instantly hard, and she couldn't miss it.

"I'm not used to being examined by a *naked* doctor," she
said, her gaze affixed to my cock.

"The scans show no injuries or imbalances in your
blood," I said, dropping the device on the small table beside
the bed.

"You said I'd be pleasured, tested for my ability to
orgasm."

Trax groaned and dropped his head to take a nipple into
his mouth.

Her eyes slid closed, and I felt her need, Trax's
satisfaction swirl between us.

"A test is not needed. Your mates are well aware of how
you can be sexually satisfied."

"Surnen, I… I need to know you're okay."

Trax lifted his head, his eyes filled with desire. I knew
what those little buds felt like on my tongue, and I ached for
my own turn. While I couldn't miss Mikki's desire, I also felt
her unease.

"There is much unsaid between us, isn't there?" I asked.

"Can you believe you only arrived yesterday?" Trax
asked her, his hand sliding absently over her belly
and hip.

Her own hand came up, brushed the integrations
around his neck and up to his ear. He didn't flinch, didn't
turn away. I felt… pride, and it pleased me that Mikki had
truly relieved Trax of his worries.

She bit her lip, uncertain. "I have made many mistakes," she admitted.

Sighing, I dropped onto the bed to sit on her other side. She was in our bed—not tied to it as I'd threatened, but between us. "You were correct, what you said. What happened to my parents had nothing to do with you being caught beneath the sea."

"I'm sorry about your family. My parents and I don't really get along, but I couldn't imagine them being gone."

"It was a long time ago," I admitted. "I shut myself off. It was... safer that way. Until you showed up. Then—"

"Bam," she said, finishing for me. It wasn't the word I'd have used, but...

"Yes. Bam. You defied me at every turn. I was determined to teach you control, to rein in your emotions. But I realize I was wrong."

"I was wrong, too. I'm sorry I fought you all the time. I understand now. I know you need to keep me safe." A blush crept up her neck, made her whole face a pretty pink. She looked away. "I will try to control myself. I don't want to freak you out by being too emotional. I'm sorry."

"Do no such thing. Your emotions make you powerful, Mikki. They make me feel alive. I need you to feel everything. I want to feel everything with you."

She pushed up onto an elbow and reached for me, touched my arm. "But Trax made me see, thirty feet underwater, that we all follow rules. I thought I didn't follow any, that I was above them."

"Your rules saved us," Trax said.

She looked over her shoulder at him. "You were so brave."

He rolled his eyes, just as I'd seen Rachel do, then

laughed. "I was desperate to prove myself worthy. I wanted to understand you, mate, to have something in common where we had none."

"Mission accomplished." Mikki fell onto her back so she could look to both of us. "I can't believe you used a log for a surfboard to get to me."

"I will see that the Academy adds swimming to its many lessons," I said, making a mental note to speak to Maxim and gain his support before contacting Vice Admiral Niobe at the Coalition Academy. She was half human, raised on Earth, and most likely had the skills required to teach recruits how to swim. Or find someone who could.

As long as it wasn't my mate. I stroked her hair, allowed the dark strands to slip between my fingers. My attentions brought her gaze back to me.

"I'm so sorry, Surnen. I defied you because I thought you were like everyone else on Earth who wanted to confine me. Decide who I should be, what I should do. I can't live like that."

"Ah, mate. Don't you see? My rules are in place to set you free."

She pushed up once again, this time all the way to her knees so she was before me, her face at the same height as mine. She stroked my hair, my cheek, studied me so closely I felt like I was under Rachel's microscope. "I promise to ask why from now on. Why do I have to follow a specific rule? Why are certain protocols in place?"

"I shall be sure to tell you the reasons."

"I shall promise never to step foot in water outside of a bathing tube ever again," Trax added.

I sensed Mikki's disappointment, and my response was

immediate. "You shall learn to swim along with the rest of us. I have a feeling Mikki will make an excellent teacher."

Trax groaned, making Mikki laugh, but I felt her joy at my words. The ocean truly was a part of her, something she would need to visit to feel whole. Perhaps, once Helion cleared Valuri of the Hive threat, we could return. If not, there were hundreds of other worlds. Surely one of them could provide for her needs.

Things weren't resolved between us. I wasn't naive enough to think that. It had barely been a day. We had the rest of our lives to work through any issue that might arise. There would be plenty of issues with a wild, free spirit like Mikki. Yet we shared a new understanding since our trip to Valuri. Things had changed, for the better.

Mikki had made me see that life was more than protocols and structure. Life was messy. It was wild. No matter how much routine I put in place, bad things happened. Good things, too.

Like our match. She was the most unexpected, unplanned thing of all.

The most important.

She slid a hand down the center of her body, cupped her pussy. "You're not done with your medical exam."

Heat flared between us. "I thought you said that it, um, didn't turn you on?" I tried to remember the Earth wording she'd used. I'd never once been aroused by a medical exam. Ever. Even when I was testing the arousal of someone else, or someone else's mate, for example. That pleasure had not been mine for the taking. I hadn't *wanted* it. It hadn't belonged to me. Mikki's desires, her sexual needs were mine to fulfill, no matter what they were. This playfulness was intriguing... and arousing.

"I'm turned on. Can't you feel me through your magical collar?"

Oh fuck, yes, I could feel how needy she was. It made me hot, too.

I gripped the base of my cock, stroked from root to tip, smearing the pre-cum with my thumb. "You want to be probed, mate? I've got a probe for you."

Her gaze fell to my cock, and she bit her lip, her hand still between her thighs.

"Yes, please."

Trax took hold of her wrist and brought her fingers to his mouth, licked them clean of her arousal. She moaned. He groaned. I growled.

Mikki was mine, and I wasn't letting her go.

———

Mikki

OH. My. God. Did he have a *probe*.

At first I'd truly wanted him to wand me or whatever it was called to allow him peace of mind that I hadn't been hurt on Valuri. I was tired, sure, but I hadn't hurt myself in any way. I knew I was well, but I wanted Surnen to believe it. Things shifted quickly though. Seeing them naked, stripped bare not just of clothing but of their darkest secrets, too, was arousing. It made them even more attractive.

It wasn't just the physical that pulled me to them, although the feel of Surnen's cock as it filled me deep, as it stretched me open, was hot as fuck. It was them. Their fierceness. Their pride. Their honor.

Trax had climbed onto a log and dropped to the bottom of a Valurian sea to save me. He'd risked his life when he'd never once been in water before. It would have been certain death for him if his helmet hadn't stopped the power of the Hive vacuum long enough for us to get to the surface.

He'd been prepared to die. For me.

After learning about what had happened to his family, I couldn't believe Surnen had given in and let me go to another planet. Then things went to shit and yeah, he'd freaked. I didn't blame him. I understood him now. Even, like he said, after such a short time.

"Mate," he murmured, kissing the curve of my ear. He held himself off me with his forearms, but thrust into me with a fervor and intensity brought on by danger.

We were alive. We were together, and he was proving it, one stroke of his huge cock at a time.

"You feel so good," I said, trying to catch my breath. I loved the collars in moments like this. Knew how Surnen felt, that he found pleasure in my body. My less than B-cups. In my petite frame. In my sassy attitude. He was getting lost in me.

So I let go. Grabbed his ass with my hands and held on. Took everything he gave to me.

"Fuck, I want to stay inside you forever," he murmured, slowing and looking down at me.

"I thought you said you were tying me to your bed and never letting me get up."

"Never letting you out of bed can be arranged," Trax said. "As for tying you up, it will be hard for us to fuck you together if we do that."

Need coursed through me, and I knew they both felt it.

The idea of taking both of them, being between them, making us one, was exactly what I wanted.

It was like the dream but better. This was my reality. "Yes. I don't want to wait."

Surnen pulled out and I whimpered, but he remained between my thighs. Both of them looked down at my pussy, now slick and open.

"We will take you between us. Fuck you. Pleasure you." Trax rolled off the bed as Surnen slipped a finger inside my pussy, over my clit. I nearly jumped off the bed.

"I thought that was only for an official claiming. You... you want to do that? Now?"

"Yes. We will fill you up. Make you beg."

I lifted my hips to get more of him. "Please," I was already begging. Why the hell were they taking so damn long?

"But it is not time to claim you, mate. It has only been a day. While I have no doubt you are mine—"

"Ours," Trax clarified.

"—we all know we have much to learn about another. I will not steal time from you, time to make your choice. Will we fuck you? Me in your pussy, Trax in your ass? Yes. Claim you? No."

The blast of arousal that came through the collars was so strong I'd have been knocked down if I weren't already sprawled on the bed. "Please," I begged again. "I want both of you. Now." I didn't care about anything else. I didn't care if it hurt. I didn't care if they tied me up, spanked me, fucked me until I collapsed. I *needed.*

"Female, you will turn me into a rebel yet. I might believe in full protocol, but I do not need to share you. I do not wish for anyone to hear your breathy whimpers, your screams of pleasure, to see your wet pussy spread open and greedy for our cocks."

"You like protocol," I said, my hips lifting and moving to Surnen's fingers. "I thought you had to claim me in front of a bunch of warriors. Don't you need to follow the rules?"

"I need *you* more." He looked to Trax. "Let's get her ready."

Before I knew what that meant, Surnen lifted me off the bed and onto his lap, chest to chest, my legs straddling him. I had to tilt my chin up to look into his face.

"Never had a cock in your ass, have you, mate?" Surnen asked, lifting me up some more so that my pussy hovered over his cock.

His golden eyes were so fair, so open to me now. Only yesterday he had been closed off. Open to me as a mate, but not open to this. To emotion. To need. To everything.

I clenched and squeezed around him, trying to adjust to him. Both of them were huge, *all over*. I had to wonder if Trax would fit back there.

"I'll get inside you, mate," Trax said as if he could read my mind. Oh yeah, the collars. "But I must ready you first."

"No vibrating plugs?" I asked, glancing at Trax over my shoulder as Surnen easily lifted me up and let gravity drop me back onto him. I gasped.

"I thought you liked the plug, mate," he said. He held it up, although I had no idea when he'd kept it. I looked at the device that had driven me wild the night before.

"I do, but it's not you."

He tilted his head, those dark eyes meeting mine. He smiled. "You'll get the plug to prepare you; then you'll get me."

Surnen fucked me, holding me still as he thrust up into

me, allowing Trax the opportunity to work the plug deep. It had been like the previous time, pressing against me there; then a gush of lubricant filled me, instantly easing the way for the device. I gasped as it went in, but it was at its smallest setting. Smaller than when they'd removed it from me the night before.

Perhaps it had done its job, for when it began to enlarge within, it didn't hurt. In fact, it felt really fucking good. And then the vibrations kicked in.

Oh. My. God.

I was going to come, and I hadn't even gotten Trax inside me yet. When I did, I wasn't sure if I would survive.

Unlike drowning at the bottom of a Valurian sea, this would be a great way to go.

———

Trax

SHE LOVED IT. I could see it in the way she writhed on Surnen's cock, felt it through the collars. Not all mates liked ass play and only took a cock there as part of the ritual claiming. Mikki would not be one of those females.

Mikki was as wild as the oceans she loved. She would want to take both of us together. Often. That worked for me.

Perhaps it was the near-death experience, or the fact that we'd revealed such dark, deep parts of ourselves so quickly after meeting each other, but I wanted to be with her, in her. With Surnen. I wanted her to know that we were with her. Inside her. Part of her.

I never, ever wanted her to doubt, to feel alone.

I had. I'd doubted myself for so long, didn't think I was worthy as more than just somebody's second. I was a second to Surnen, but Mikki had proven I wasn't the extra mate to *her*. She was the only one whose opinion mattered. No one else.

She wasn't repulsed by my integrations. She didn't care that I'd rarely touched a planet's surface. That I had no idea how to swim, to surf, to be like her.

Mikki wanted me. *Me!*

I felt it. Knew it couldn't be a lie because of the collars. Her desire for me was truth. Her need for me, as Trax, not a second Prillon warrior, was truth.

That and that alone had saved me. I might have died in a stupid ocean, but I'd been saved emotionally. Then she went right on saving me.

If Mikki wanted us to fuck her together, I wasn't denying any of us that pleasure.

While Surnen kissed her, cupped her ass and lifted and lowered her on his cock, the plug did its job. Lubricating her well so she could take my cock easily, opening her up so it wouldn't hurt when I did so and arousing her to the point of mindlessness. Until the pleasure was so great that she came.

Her scream of pleasure was probably heard as far away as the transport room, but I didn't care. I was proud to know we were good mates to her, ensuring she was well satisfied. And I hadn't even gotten inside her yet.

While she was still coming down from her orgasm, I carefully removed the plug from her, tossed it aside.

Her head was on Surnen's chest, her eyes closed. Sweat dampened her skin. Her hair clung to her cheeks. I looked to Surnen, and he nodded, spread his knees wider, which gave me room to move closer.

I couldn't miss the way her pussy opened around the base of Surnen's cock, the way her back entrance was relaxed and slick, ready for me. Leaning forward, I kissed her shoulder. Gripping the base of my cock, I lined up with her virgin hole, pressed in.

Her eyes opened, and while she didn't move, she watched me. I kept my gaze fixed on hers as I pushed deep. Slowly, carefully. Stilled and waited.

All at once, the ring of muscle gave way and the head of my cock popped into her.

She groaned and clung to Surnen. He spoke to her, whispered words of praise as I inched slowly into her. She was hot and so fucking tight, my balls ached. The plug had done its job, making her unbearably slick inside. Still I was cautious, entering her slowly to give her time to adjust to being filled with two cocks. Two big, Prillon cocks.

When I was finally in all the way, when she was pretty much sitting on both our laps, we began to move. Surnen cupped her breasts. I slid my hands up and down her back, then gripped her hips, watched as my cock moved in and out of her stretched hole.

The collars told me everything I needed to know. She loved it. Was aroused by it. In fact, she was close to coming again. That need, swirled with Surnen's own pleasure and mine, was unlike anything I'd ever felt before. More powerful than any orgasm we'd had the night before.

"It's so good," she moaned. "Oh God."

Her eyes were closed, and she gripped and held, shook and arched her back, unsure of what to do. Between us, there wasn't much she could do but feel. Surrender. Submit.

And she did. From one breath to the next, she came.

"Fuck," Surnen growled.

Holy shit. I couldn't hold back, not with the way her pussy and ass were clenching down. I came hard, spurt after spurt of cum filling her. Surnen came as well. No way could he have held off.

I was blinded by pleasure. The air was filled with our breathy groans and cries of satisfaction, the scent of fucking. Our ragged breaths.

"Perfect, mate," I said finally. "Beautiful, perfect Mikki."

Mikki was catching her breath, but the corner of her mouth tipped up in a small smile.

Carefully I pulled out—even though I wanted to stay buried within her forever—and dropped onto the bed. Surnen lifted her off him and set her on top of me, her small body like a blanket draped over my chest. I could feel her breathing, her heat.

Surnen went to the bathing room and quickly returned with a wet cloth, cleaned our mate between her sticky, cum-coated thighs. I cleaned up as well and tossed it to the floor as Surnen climbed onto the bed beside us.

"I think you were right, Surnen," she murmured. I felt her satisfaction and her weariness.

She'd transported not once, but twice today, survived a near-death experience with the Hive and then had been well and truly fucked. She'd sleep for a while.

"What's that, mate?"

"Staying here in bed is the best idea ever. Let's make it a rule."

With that, she fell asleep, and I followed soon after. I was at peace, our mate with us. Satisfied. Safe. Surrounded.

I couldn't have been happier.

EPILOGUE

M ikki, *Twenty-six days later, The Colony garden*

THE DRESS WAS WHITE. White to symbolize that I was prepared to be "painted" the color of my husband's family. If my grandmother had still been alive, she would have been disappointed that I did not wear a traditional *shiromuku,* the old-fashioned Shinto marriage kimono. I was born and raised in Hawaii, though, and my parents were fluid in their beliefs.

It was odd that the symbolism of adopting a mate's colors was practiced on Prillon Prime as well. Two worlds, literally, but that one tradition was the same. I'd told Surnen the very day I met him that I would not wear gray, his family color. Looking back, it had been an ignorant thing to say. I'd been ruthless and laser focused in what I'd expected of a match. It had been all about me. *Me, me, me.* Then everything fell apart. Then I learned that although Surnen and Trax might each be the size of a VW bug, they had feelings, insecurities, emotions. They bled just like me. And with my stupid words about the color gray, I'd hurt Surnen. I was fixing that now.

"Are you ready?" Rachel handed me three branches from the Chinese banyan tree that grew in my family's backyard in Hawaii. Each branch was about a foot long, decorated with white ribbon, and there was one for each of us. My mother had planted the tree when she and my father moved into our family home, and it was now taller than the roof. I missed that tree. I missed my parents. I was happy here on The Colony. Very, very happy.

I looked her way. "I owe you, Rachel. Big-time."

She smiled. "Oh, I know. Trust me."

For the past twenty-four days, Trax, Surnen and I had spoken of the claiming. We all wanted it but had chosen to wait almost the full thirty days. We'd agreed to an Earth ceremony to go along with the traditional Prillon claiming —minus the public sex part—from the very start. But Rachel had helped me make a few changes in secret. Changes that I had wanted to make it special for Surnen and Trax.

"You are so beautiful, Umiko. So beautiful." My mother's voice carried from the comm screen and through the garden area. I lifted the tree branches she'd sent to me in gratitude.

"Thank you, Mother. I am so happy you and Father are here to share this with me."

My father, looking stern as always, nodded gruffly. They sat side by side on the familiar couch in their living room. "We are honored, Daughter, to meet your husband."

"About that, I should probably explain..." I laughed out loud, which made my mother smile and my father frown.

He was very much like Surnen, raised that showing strong emotion to others was inconsiderate. Maintaining control was a way of showing care and compassion to others. I had never understood the depths of emotion that swam beneath the surface of his fierce expression until Surnen and the mating collars. After that I realized my father was most likely a volcano under an ice cap. I'd never taken the time to understand him and wouldn't have realized how my father ticked without my uncompromising and protocol-driven mate. *Surnen*. One more reason I loved him.

Trax and Surnen chose that moment to enter the garden wearing their wedding garb. For Surnen, a tunic and pants in steel gray, his family colors. Trax looked equally impressive in blue lined with silver, his old family colors bordered by the new. The Prillons were not without traditions, but they still had nothing on my Japanese grandparents. I remembered drinking tea with my grandmother, and every item had a proper place on the tray, from the sugar to the spoon. I'd loved her so much, and those times were precious memories that I hoped to recreate someday with my own children.

"Are you unwell?" Trax reached me first, his hands cupping my face and lifting my chin so I looked at him. "I feel your sadness, mate."

Surnen settled his hands on my hips from behind and pulled me to him so my back made contact with his chest. "We both feel your pain and longing. You asked us to remain in the corridor until summoned, but we were unable to comply with your request. You will not suffer while you are mine."

So bossy. So pushy. So... perfect.

"That's about to be forever," I reminded.

He lowered his lips to my ear and growled softly. "Exactly my point, female."

My father chose that moment to clear his throat and assert his presence—even from several light-years away—and disapproval. "Umiko."

Surnen stiffened at my father's tone, and I felt his cold, protective fury like an ice bath through my veins. I'd heard that tone of voice more times than I could count, but Trax froze, looked down at me with a question in his eyes, and grinned. He sensed Surnen's tension, too. I looked to him and he winked. "This should be fun."

My primary male released me and stepped toward the screen that he had apparently either not noticed when he entered the garden area or had chosen to ignore. I wasn't sure which. "Dr. Tanaka."

His voice was pure steel, but Surnen bowed slightly at the waist, then turned to face my mother. "Mrs. Tanaka." He bowed again. "I am Dr. Surnen Syrzon of Prillon Prime, and your daughter, Mikki, is my matched mate. I am honored to meet you both and wish you to know that I love your daughter and will serve and protect her until the day I die. My life and my heart are hers, as she is mine."

My mother blinked, slowly, taking in the scene. She looked to the hand Trax held to the small of my back, and I saw the calculations begin. My father ignored me and Trax completely to scowl at Surnen. My mate was sized up, dismissed in silence, and my father returned his gaze to me through the huge screen that Rachel had somehow managed to bring to the garden.

"Umiko—"

"She has asked you repeatedly to call her Mikki."
Surnen dared to correct my father.

"You will explain yourself," my father said, his voice and
image so clear it was as if I could reach out and touch him.
Yet he was so far away. "We hired a new attorney to appeal
your case. You would have been free in a matter of weeks.
Why are you not on Earth? And why did you not tell your
mother your plans to volunteer to be a bride? You did not
even say good-bye."

His voice broke on the last, and I felt tears burning
behind my eyelids. In all my life, I had never seen my father
cry. He would not blink, his dark eyes full of emotions I was
shocked to see shimmering behind unshed tears.

"You hired an attorney? You didn't tell me." I stepped
away from Trax and walked toward the screen, shock
making me feel numb. "I was sentenced to ten years, and
you didn't even come to court. Not once."

"Your mother sent an attorney to witness the
proceedings and keep us informed," he shared.

I stared at him, my mouth open.

"What?" My mother sent an attorney to sit in the
courtroom for them? Hardly. No. No way. "Mother doesn't
know any lawyers. It was you."

"Your mother was concerned for your welfare," he
continued.

Damn it. Even now he couldn't admit that he had been
worried. That he loved me, too. That he was the one who'd
been scared for me.

"You are a male of honor. I thank you for taking such
care with your daughter." Surnen assured my father and
stepped to my side, placing his hand at the small of my back
in a move that had my mother's eyes going wide as Trax had

moved forward and still touched me as well. I was between them, right where I wanted to be. Two huge warriors flanking me, protecting me. They'd always be by my side. I knew it after we'd transported off Valuri, and it had been validated every day since.

I looked up at Trax, then to Surnen. He meant every word he said, which only made me very confused. And hurt. "What are you talking about, Surnen? They weren't even there!"

During the trial, I had felt every emotion I could name and a few I couldn't. Abandonment. Betrayal. Hurt. Fear. Confusion. I'd been terrified of going to jail. I'd felt regret over the choices I'd made in my life. Ashamed that I'd dishonored my family. My heart had broken over and over in that courtroom, and Surnen was *thanking* my parents for not being there for me? Was he insane?

I felt him through the collar. His emotions were calm, approving. "Your father knows you, Mikki," Surnen replied. "He understood that if he or your mother were present in the courtroom, you would have broken down. It would have been much more difficult for you to survive the process without losing control—which would have made you even more miserable. His care for you assured that you survived and became stronger, rather than broken and weak. He knows you well and gave you the space you needed to become resilient."

"Oh my God," I whispered.

I couldn't move. All I could do was relive every moment in that courtroom and imagine what it would have been like staring at my worried mother's or my stern father's faces in the crowd. Surnen was right. I would have lost it. I would have been sobbing. It would have been... horrible.

"He is correct, mate," Trax murmured. His thumb slid up and down along my spine in a small gesture of reassurance.

My mother cleared her throat, and both of my mates straightened, which made them ten times more adorable in my eyes. Mother was even smaller than me, and yet they snapped to attention as if they were responding to Prime Nial himself.

"We miss you, Mikki," Mother admitted. "We love you. We want you to come home." She took a deep breath and looked from Surnen to Trax and back to me. "Even if I didn't know the rules for the Brides Program, I suspect that is no longer possible."

"No, it is not." Trax's hand slid up my back to settle on my shoulder in a gesture my parents couldn't miss. Surnen may have introduced himself as my mate, but Trax was staking his claim just the same. "Your daughter honors us by choosing us as her mates. We will spend our lives honoring and protecting her."

With Surnen on my left, I was surrounded by love, acceptance and pride. They were proud to stand with me, to meet my parents.

"Both of you?" My mother blinked hard. Twice.

I'd known, ever since Valuri, that I wouldn't reject the match, that I wanted Surnen and Trax. We'd agreed to wait, to just... be for a time. They hadn't let me out of our quarters for three days once we'd returned from Valuri. While I hadn't been tied to the bed the whole time, they'd used restraints for some seriously sexy times. I hadn't minded one bit. Since then, they'd shown me all of Base 3—and I'd learned to appreciate the desert a bit, although the rocks would never replace the ocean in my heart. But I'd spent time with the other Earth women and even gotten to know their bossy mates. Any mention of Valuri was met by growls from my mates and even the governor.

The last I'd heard, I.C. had taken over the investigation of the Hive vacuum things, and that was all. Trax had said they were very secretive about their investigations, so it was possible we'd never know what those machines were, even if he and I had had the closest encounter with them. On the plus side, Rachel, Surnen and I had been invited by Prime Nial to join a new task force looking for anomalies on uninhabited planets like Valuri. Surnen was usually busy helping with more urgent matters, and Rachel was more about the chemistry, so that left me to send out probes, collect data and analyze the ecosystems. It was fascinating work—and there were literally thousands of planets out there the Coalition Fleet hadn't set foot on. Thousands. Maybe millions. Enough work for a lifetime.

During the past few weeks, I'd also connected with my parents, as my mates had suggested, going so far as to ask my mother for the Banyon branches for today. She'd known I was getting married to an alien... but I hadn't exactly told her *everything*. "Mikki?"

"Mother, Father, this is Surnen, my primary mate." Even though Surnen had introduced himself, they needed me to confirm his words. I glanced up at Surnen, who dipped his chin in acknowledgment.

"And this is Trax, my second mate." I looked up at Trax, who nodded as well and grinned at my mother with that heart-stopping, boyish, irresistible grin that always made me give him whatever the hell he wanted, which was usually me taking my clothes off. "They are both my mates, and I love them very much. I am marrying them today as in

Earth custom, then will be participating in a Prillon claiming ceremony."

I felt Surnen's pride and satisfaction. Yes, he was eager to claim me in the Prillon way, although we'd agreed to do it in private, leaving out the public display. I'd changed my mind about that, but neither of them knew it yet. It was to be my surprise. The way I could feel their eagerness to finally make me theirs, to have the collars change from black to gray, only validated my decision.

"I wanted you both to be here, at my wedding," I told my parents.

I opened my arms to encompass the garden area on Base 3. The green space had been started by the other brides and was located in the middle of The Colony base, kind of like Central Park in New York, except under a supersized dome. The garden was beautiful, an odd mix of plants from Earth and other worlds, and the warriors who lived here had adopted it as their own. They tended the plants and trees with great care.

I now had two of my own trees to add to the garden and would ask the warriors to plant them later. The trees had been transported from Earth, again with Rachel's help. One special tree for each of my mates stood behind me in large pots. One Chinese banyan from Hawaii and one sakaki tree from Japan, in honor of my grandparents. I had draped the trees in white and steel-gray ribbon.

My father wiped a tear from each cheek with the back of his thumb and nodded gruffly. "Mikki, you are my daughter. You will always be my daughter." He looked to Surnen. "I will give my blessing for this marriage on the condition that Mikki's mother and I are allowed to visit her at least twice each year."

Surnen bowed again, lower this time. "Of course. I will personally schedule your transport to The Colony. Your government does not allow citizens of Prillon Prime to visit Earth, but you are welcome here."

"My daughter is from Earth," Father stated.

"Not anymore," Surnen clarified. "As my mate, she is an official citizen of Prillon Prime."

"I see." My father cleared his throat. "Mikki, does this marriage make you happy?"

I nodded. "Yes, Father. I love them both, very much. I am very happy here." I smiled, the first real, huge, happy smile I'd felt since walking out here. It hadn't been love at first sight. Far from it. All three of us had walls erected around our hearts. Protecting them, keeping them safe from further harm. We'd all been wounded, not just physically but emotionally too. I was thankful for the mess that had happened on Valuri, for I doubted that any of us would have let down our guards, let our true selves appear if not for what we'd endured. It had bared us to each other. That exposure, that *truth* was what gave us the power to heal. To love.

Trax leaned down and kissed me. Gently. Sweetly. I felt his love, his happiness through the collars as he did so.

My father cleared his throat. Trax lifted his head and smiled at me. I laughed, then looked back at my parents.

They were coming to visit. They weren't freaking out about me marrying two aliens, and I'd made peace with my feelings for my father. No, that wasn't right. I saw him differently now. Understood him, which made all my anger and upset I'd had for him in the past slip away.

He truly was very much like Surnen.

"Good." Father looked from Surnen to Trax several

times. "You will see to her care and happiness. I love my daughter and will not accept ill treatment of her."

Trax nodded. "You have our word. Mikki is our world now."

"Very well. I give my blessing."

My mother smiled and leaned into his side. They sat in the living room of the home I'd grown up in. She lifted a cell phone from her lap and typed in a message to someone. Who, I had no idea, until a loud whooping noise sounded on the other end and a barrage of people swarmed onto the screen to surround my parents. My cousins, aunts, uncles, friends from school, even a couple of my closest coworkers at SynGen. They all shouted and whistled, and I burst into tears as I realized the truth.

Fate had not given me perfect parents, but the exact parents I needed to become who I was now. Standing on another world, prepared to begin a new life. If they had been different, I would not be who I was today. I would not be as strong. As wild. As happy with my new life.

Surnen's arm went around my back, and he kissed the top of my head.

It took me a little bit to pull myself together. "Hi, everyone."

A chorus of greetings, shouts, whistles and encouragement came through the screen as Governor Maxim moved to stand slightly off to the side so as not to impede anyone's view. Rachel grinned and handed him a small piece of paper. "I hope this is okay," she said to me. "I wasn't sure what to go with, so I just went with the tried and true."

Maxim cleared his throat. "We are gathered here today to witness the joining of three people, Umiko—"

"Mikki. Call her Mikki," my father interrupted, and I laughed through my tears as he smiled at me, really smiled, like he'd pulled off the best surprise party of the century. He probably had.

"We are gathered here today to witness the joining of three people, Mikki Tanaka of Earth with Dr. Surnen Syrzon and Warrior Trax Lorvarz of Prillon Prime, whose hearts and spirits are entwined as one. If anyone knows of any reason why these three should not be joined, speak now or forever hold your peace."

Surnen literally stood so straight he appeared to be several inches taller. "Do not dare speak."

The command was for everyone, but Trax burst into laughter. "That's not the point."

"I do not care what the point is. Mikki is mine."

My father chuckled, a sound I could not remember hearing since I was a child. "Oh, Daughter, I am coming to visit you soon. I cannot wait to meet your husbands."

The ceremony was over quickly, ending with the traditional kissing of the bride... times two. I said goodbye to my parents with Rachel promising to hand them off to a transport officer to schedule their first visit.

After that, Rachel and Maxim left as well. This was what Surnen and Trax expected, to be left alone to do the traditional claiming in private. It was finally time to reveal my secret, to give them what they wanted, what they needed to know I truly belonged to them. I would not deny them this. I couldn't deny them anything.

It felt amazing being married to these huge warriors, but it wasn't what mattered to them. This ceremony had been for me. I wanted to respect their custom, their traditions so they had no doubt this was a done deal. I belonged to them in all ways. As they watched, I shimmied out of my dress, letting the soft material pool at my feet. I was left in a sexy negligee I'd had Rachel help me create on the S-Gen machine. It had thin straps to hold it up, but the silk dipped into a plunging V that barely covered my breasts. Lace hid my nipples from their view... barely. It stopped high on my thighs, my ass barely covered. I wore nothing beneath but gray garters and matching, thigh-high stockings. All the important bits were...available for their pleasure. And mine.

"Mate," Trax growled.

"You said you would not wear gray," Surnen said, his gaze raking over every inch of me.

I nodded. "I said a lot of things before I knew you. I'm proud to wear your family's colors." I ran my hand over the silk. "Here." Lifting my hand to the collar, I added, "And soon here."

Rachel had said lingerie and sexy underthings weren't the Prillon way. They liked their women naked, no need for any kind of covering to get them all hot and bothered. Still, lust spiked through the collars, and I knew Surnen and Trax were *very* pleased with what I wore. Perhaps just as much because of the color as for the barely there styling. I held up a hand to keep my two mates at arm's length.

"Not yet, mates. You have not properly claimed me in a Prillon mating ceremony."

Both frowned down at me.

"We have agreed to forgo this tradition at your request, mate." Surnen looked confused, but his cock knew exactly what it wanted. Me. Like now. I couldn't miss the way either of their cocks were thickly outlined in their uniform pants.

I was having trouble standing before them with their caveman need to claim me hitting me through the collar.

I reached down to the planting border where I'd hidden a dark gray cape and draped it over my shoulders. Tipping my chin back, I looked up at my big, brawny mates. "You came to me in a cape just like this one. You said it was custom. Tradition. I wear one now to honor you, to honor what we will become. Would you not feel better about protecting me if we followed the strict Prillon custom of a formal claiming before warriors sworn to us?"

Surnen actually sputtered. "Of course, but—"

"I agree," I replied quickly. "Protocol and tradition matter to you, mate. And so they matter to me."

"We can claim you privately. The collars will change to gray and our mating will be official. You were so adamant about not wanting witnesses. We honor that. There is no need for an audience, for the traditional custom." Surnen wasn't getting the message, not yet. Maybe his mind was too clouded with lust. The thought made me grin, and I knew if I could see myself in the mirror, the look would be naughty times ten.

Trax tipped his head to the side, studied me. "What are you saying, Mikki?" He seemed to be catching on faster than Surnen, but then this leap in logic was a big one, especially for me, when I'd been adamant before that I would *not* allow Surnen and Trax to fuck me in front of a roomful of chanting warriors. I'd said a lot of things I'd changed my mind about.

"I want you both," I continued. "I want this to be perfect, not just for me, but for you as well. I want you to feel like you've done everything you could to protect me. I'm willing to compromise too, especially when it comes to your customs and traditions. I know you will do anything to keep me safe and happy, and I accept that this is what you need to feel like you are doing that."

When they both just stared at me, I turned and walked away. They would follow, I had no doubt.

They did and I smiled. I heard their heavy footsteps, even on the soft ground. We approached the central room Maxim had set aside for our claiming ceremony. The low rumble of male voices chanting grew louder and louder.

"Mikki?" Surnen stopped me with a gentle hand on my shoulder, turning me to face him. "As Trax said, this is not necessary."

I looked up at the mate I loved, felt everything he had inside him. "Yes, it is. I am taking care of you, too, you know. I want this. I want you to claim me the proper way, so everyone knows you are mine." I reached for Trax's hand and pulled him close as well. "I want them to know that I choose you. Both of you. You're mine and I'm never giving you up."

They were both speechless, so I pulled them along behind me and smiled at a guard that had been placed outside the door. He opened the door for us with a solemn nod, and I knew this ceremony wasn't just for show; it was sacred, an oath between warriors to protect and defend the females they chose for their own.

Around the room there were warriors I recognized and some I did not. I had trusted Maxim to know who Surnen and Trax would have chosen.

Walking to the center of the room, I spoke slowly and clearly so every male would hear my claim.

"I am Umiko Tanaka of Earth, and I claim the warriors Surnen and Trax as my own."

I wasn't expecting an answer, but I got one anyway, from

the entire group that stood around the edges of the room speaking in unison. "May the gods witness and protect you."

I dropped the cape, and my mates could hold back no longer. They were on me before I could even blink. They touched me. Kissed me. Fucked me. Claimed me. They said their words and I accepted their claim, as they knew I would. Surnen in my pussy, Trax claiming my ass so I was once again between them. Connecting us, making us one. I knew the moment my collar turned gray, for Surnen's eyes blazed like a golden sun as he filled me, eyes on the collar, on the sexy gray lace and satin I still wore. As they made me scream, I wanted every warrior there as witness to know that I already had gods protecting me. Two of them. And they were mine. All mine. Forever.

***

Thank you for reading Her Cyborg Warriors. Did you miss Cyborg's Secret Baby?

Atlan Warlord Jorik guards the Coalition Fleet's Processing Center on Earth, protecting warriors and brides without mercy or distraction...until he sees Gabriela. She is everything the beast within him craves. Soft. Curved. Unafraid. He dreams of courting her properly, wooing her into accepting his beast's claim, and making her his—body and soul. Danger strikes and his beast takes control—resulting in his immediate removal from Earth. From Gabriela.

Gabriela fell in love with an alien Warlord who fought to

save her life, then disappeared, only to learn he was later killed in a battle with the Hive. She moves on with her life as best she can, with one beautiful reminder of their time together. A baby.

When she learns Jorik isn't dead, but banished to the Colony, she and the baby are sent to find him. The problem? He's not just contaminated, he's been newly matched by the Interstellar Brides Program. And not to her.

Get Cyborg's Secret Baby NOW!

A SPECIAL THANK YOU TO MY READERS...

Want more? I've got *hidden* bonus content on my web site *exclusively* for those on my mailing list.

If you are already on my email list, you don't need to do a thing! Simply scroll to the bottom of my newsletter emails and click on the *super-secret* link.

Not a member? What are you waiting for? In addition to ALL of my bonus content (great new stuff will be added regularly) you will be the first to hear about my newest release the second it hits the stores—AND you will get a free book as a special welcome gift.

Sign up now! http://freescifiromance.com

FIND YOUR INTERSTELLAR MATCH!

YOUR mate is out there. Take the test today and discover your perfect match. Are you ready for a sexy alien mate (or two)?

VOLUNTEER NOW!

interstellarbridesprogram.com

DO YOU LOVE AUDIOBOOKS?

Grace Goodwin's books are now available as
audiobooks...everywhere.

LET'S TALK SPOILER ROOM!

Interested in joining my **Sci-Fi Squad**? Meet new like-minded sci-fi romance fanatics and chat with Grace! Get excerpts, cover reveals and sneak peeks before anyone else. Be part of a private Facebook group that shares pictures and fun news! Join here:

https://www.facebook.com/groups/scifisquad/

***

Want to talk about Grace Goodwin books with others? Join the **SPOILER ROOM** and spoil away! Your GG BFFs are waiting! (And so is Grace)

Join here:

https://www.facebook.com/groups/ggspoilerroom/

GET A FREE BOOK!

JOIN MY MAILING LIST TO BE THE FIRST TO KNOW OF NEW RELEASES, FREE BOOKS, SPECIAL PRICES AND OTHER AUTHOR GIVEAWAYS.

http://freescifiromance.com

ALSO BY GRACE GOODWIN

Mated to the Cyborgs

Cyborg Seduction

Her Cyborg Beast

Cyborg Fever

Rogue Cyborg

Cyborg's Secret Baby

Her Cyborg Warriors

Interstellar Brides® Program: The Virgins

The Alien's Mate

His Virgin Mate

Claiming His Virgin

His Virgin Bride

His Virgin Princess

Interstellar Brides® Program: Ascension Saga

Ascension Saga, book 1

Ascension Saga, book 2

Ascension Saga, book 3

Trinity: Ascension Saga - Volume 1

Ascension Saga, book 4

Ascension Saga, book 5

Ascension Saga, book 6

Faith: Ascension Saga - Volume 2

Ascension Saga, book 7

Ascension Saga, book 8

Ascension Saga, book 9

Destiny: Ascension Saga - Volume 3

Other Books

Their Conquered Bride

Wild Wolf Claiming: A Howl's Romance

ABOUT GRACE

Grace Goodwin is a USA Today and international bestselling author of Sci-Fi and Paranormal romance with more than one million books sold. Grace's titles are available worldwide in multiple languages in ebook, print and audio formats. Two best friends, one left-brained, the other right-brained, make up the award-winning writing duo that is Grace Goodwin.

They are both mothers, escape room enthusiasts, avid readers and intrepid defenders of their preferred beverages. (There may or may not be an ongoing tea vs. coffee war occurring during their daily communications.) Grace loves to hear from readers!

All of Grace's books can be read as sexy, stand-alone adventures. But be careful, she likes her heroes hot and her love scenes hotter. You have been warned...

www.gracegoodwin.com
gracegoodwinauthor@gmail.com

Printed in Poland
by Amazon Fulfillment
Poland Sp. z o.o., Wrocław

55986996R00123